CW01508697

The Weight of Sin

Ray Canham
2024

Published by Earth Island Books
Pickforde Lodge
Pickforde Lane
Ticehurst
East Sussex
TN5 7BN

www.earthislandbooks.com

Paperback ISBN 9781916864320
ebook ISBN 9781916864337

Printed and bound by Solopress

Dedication

This book is dedicated to the Isle of Mull.
Our home for seven glorious years and
where we long to return.

The Weight of Sin

Introduction

2024

Looking back over this collection, I can see that I have a fondness for the little person, the meek and the anonymous. The chap in the corner minding their own business while everyone else swirls around in the dance of life, or the shy woman watching as the energy and excitement of other peoples lives pass her by.

I can identify with them, the introverted loners on the edge observing and over thinking. Unlike the characters who inhabit my stories though my dark side comes out on paper and not, well, you'll have to see, but be assured their lives are not all sticky buns and lashings of fizzy pop.

A few of these stories are set in the past. As such there may be some language that might feel uncomfortable these days. I decided authenticity was important, especially considering the journey the characters are on, so this is not an excuse or an apology, just a statement of fact.

Contents

Ray Canham

Burton Coggles

SPEECHES, JOKES, TOASTS

Don't fret, send SAE NOW!
FREE samples

I was on the wireless a long time ago. Burton Coggles, the Chipper Chappie.

You didn't start out on the airwaves, you had to earn that by treading the boards. I toured the theatres and playhouses up and down the country, from big halls with packed galleries and the twinkling of jewels in the spotlights from the boxes, to working men's clubs and half empty seaside shows with sticky floors and children running up and down the aisles.

Some of the bigger stars only wanted to play in the big city halls, once they had appeared in a film or two, they got too big for their boots.

I'd play them all though. The holiday places, the factory shutdown weeks around the coast, the charity appearance for the sanitorium. That's where your audience was, the housewife stuck at home all day raising the kiddies, the chap trudging into the factory day after day to support them. They paid your bills with honest money.

'*Good evening ladies and gentlemen. Testing 1,2, 4...testing 1,2, 4...hey is this microphone leaking, where's the 3 gone? Talking of number three, I learnt an interesting fact today, did you know ladies and gents, did you know that there are only three types of people in the world? In the whole world three types...those who can count and those who can't...'*

Even when I played the big London theatres, and I played them all, I was playing to the Gods, the people in the cheap seats peering down around the pillars and columns. With the lights down you couldn't see further than a couple of rows into the stalls so that was where you got your interaction from. But look up into the spotlights and you were embracing the galleries in all their faded glory.

What you wanted was to court the regulars who saved up the loose change from their wage packets and pin money for a special night out. The people in the scuffed seats with cigarette holes in and arms worn down to a shine, stacked on top of each other amidst the sticky floors and peeling statues. They were your bread and butter.

'I used to walk the plank, we couldn't afford a dog.
'Then when we got one, he kept chasing people on a bike, so we took his bike away.'

I never did off colour stuff. A bit

cheeky maybe, well, the old dears love that. I left the mucky stuff to others and the late-night reviews. I tried a few, in the early days when the money was tight. It was all a bit seedy for my tastes.

'A husband and wife had a bitter quarrel on the day of their 40th wedding anniversary.

The husband yells, "When you die, I'm getting you a headstone that reads, 'Here Lies My Wife – Cold As Ever.'"

"Really" she replies. "When you die, I'm getting you a headstone that reads, 'Here Lies My Husband – Stiff At Last.'"

When I started out, I was too young to understand. I was only 13.

We were in Southend on holiday. Five nights in a room in a guest house. Out by 10am, back in at 4pm. Landlady with a face like thunder. Even if it was pouring down, she'd not unlock the door until the clock struck 4. Not a second earlier.

That year my mother and me were huddled in the porch dripping wet. We'd been to a show, a brass band down by the pier, then the heavens opened and we ran for home and arrived 10 minutes early.

Anyway, at 4pm on the dot she opens the door.

'Cor blimey misses' I said, it's raining cats and dogs out there...I should know, I just stepped in a poodle...'

She almost cracked a smile. Ma scolded me for being cheeky, but then told me she'd seen a poster up and she had an idea, to enter me in a talent show.

I was a restless boy, always talking back. Got me into trouble at school until Mr Gethins put me on the stage. School plays and compering the school awards night came naturally to a cheeky chops like me.

So, the show comes around, there I am, backstage at the Pavilion in Southend, short trousers, jacket, and a tie borrowed from our landlady's husband. I've got my material worked out in my school exercise book...

'Ladies and Gentlemen, our next act is only 13 years old...please give a warm welcome to Master Burton Coggles.'

'Good afternoon Ladies and Gentlemen.
'It's lovely to be here in Southend. I'm here with my mother on holiday. My father couldn't join us. He's doing time...
'No, no, no not like that... he's a clock maker.

'*He's tired all the time, well he would be, he works round the clock...*

'*Always seems to have time on his hands though...*'

Goodness knows how with that material but I won!

First prize was two bob and a letter of introduction to a London agency.

Back home I put on my best whistle and flute and there I was, 14 now and all shiny, standing in the office of Dickie 'Mr. Showbiz' Sussman.

Agent to the stars it said on his card. Mostly has-beens as it turned out, the old guard who'd been forced out by the talking pictures and the variety acts, who would pad out the bill for the star attractions.

He came with my mother to a show at school. I did a turn, opened with my fatty Philomena routine...

'*She's so fat, she fell and rocked herself to sleep trying to get up!*

'*Honestly, she has more chins than China.*

'*No, really, we mustn't make fun of her, she's already got enough on her plate...*'

Then some scenery fell over. Great big bang and crash in the middle of my story.

'Ooh, that'll be her on her way down the stairs now...look out Mr Gethins, best hide your barley sugars...'

Dickie took my Ma and me to a Lyons corner house. Right on the Strand it was. All glittery and waitresses in uniforms. Ma looked uncomfortable but Dickie was a real charmer.

To her.

To me, he said my timing was off, material second rate at best and I looked like a tramp dressed up for a bar-mitzvah.

I wanted the ground to open and swallow me. I couldn't say anything because I was fighting back tears.

Then he told me my improvising was spot on, that I had something, a quick wit and even though my jokes were appalling people liked me because I smiled and sounded cheerful. He said the old dears would adore me.

My mother cried because she was proud and cried because she was afraid and she cried because I'd be away with Dickie's variety show.

'I went to this posh place the other day – the Pelican Cafe...

The food was good but the bill was enormous!'

Dickie turned up at the front door the following Saturday and asked for my father. He had to sign the papers. Pa wasn't a watch maker. He had repaired clocks and watches, but the war changed him. He came back to find his hands shaking too much to do the delicate work.

He had a small pension, but Ma had to work two cleaning jobs and take in laundry while he just sat staring at the fire we often couldn't afford coal for.

She saved up bits and bobs for our holiday, plus a little she had put away after her sister died in an explosion at the munitions factory. Pa refused to come away with us, said he hadn't earned it, but told us to have a nice time.

When we were getting ready to leave for the train he shook my hand, told me to be a good boy for my Ma, pressed two crown into my hand and ruffled my hair. Then he pecked my ma on the cheek, gave her a sort of half-hearted hug and carried her case to the cab.

'We arrive at this guest house, Duncleaning I think it was called.
"Please may we have a room?" my ma

askes the landlady.

"Certainly, with a bath or shower?"

'*Well, money is a bit tight, so she asks what the difference is?*

"You have to stand in the shower," says the landlady.'

I never saw my father again. We came back to a cold house and a note on the mantlepiece telling Ma to get Dr. Stephens and not to go in the woodshed.

No one knew he'd kept his service revolver.

'*I hate going to funerals, I'm not a mourning person.*'

Money was even tighter after that, so Dickie's offer was a godsend really.

I became Bertie Coggles, The Cheeky Cherub. Third on after the compere, Kirk Smeaton and the Sally Preston dancers.

'*I tell you what, on the way here I saw a lady drop her purse. Right outside the Regal.*

'*So, I ran after her waving and shouting to her, but she jumped on the number 41.*

'*I ran after the bus and caught up with it two stops later.*

'*Well, by now I was out of breath, panting like a dog I was.*

'I climbed up the stairs puffing and huffing and I said to her...

"Excuse me madam, but you dropped your purse on the floor outside the Regal."

"Thank you so much" she said, "Where is it?"

"I just told you, on the floor outside the Regal."'

I left school to go on tour. My Ma wasn't too happy about it, but it paid more than the factories and certainly more than being in school, and what with Pa gone the money was a necessity.

I spent three years with Dickies little troupe. The Cheeky Cherub. Eight minutes a set to two houses a day with Mondays off.

'I went to the doctors the other day.

'He said, "what's wrong with you Burton?"

'I said, "well Doctor, I have a carrot up my nose, a cucumber in one ear and a radish in the other."

He said "Well, Burton, I can see your problem...You're not eating properly!"'

The troupe became my second family.

The women looked after me, made sure my clothes were washed, I had a seat on the train and didn't miss my connections. Dickie made sure I had a cab from my Ma's house to the station or theatre. As a 14-year-old I felt important, like the star I wasn't.

The men were usually kind. I found out early on the best approach was to know my place. I wasn't the name in lights, the person they paid to see. I was the boy. The young pretender there to learn the ropes.

If my act went down badly and I walked off to a polite smattering of applause halfway through my allotted time the women put their arms around me and told me it'd be fine next time, the men offered advice, 'say this, don't say that, try this', and so on. The one thing they all said was that it had happened to them and to keep going.

The compere was Kirk Smeaton. He was an old pro who knew how to get the audience going. A few jokes, a song and a dance, always dapper. Tuxedo shiny from being pressed after being folded in a suitcase, shirt with a fresh collar every night, cufflinks and a tortoiseshell cigarette holder. Shoes shined and moustache waxed. A right charmer he was.

He read out messages after the interval, birthday wishes or wedding anniversaries, occasionally an engagement or marriage and he had a joke or song for every occasion.

'Big hand for Mr & Mrs Bloom, Stan and Irene ladies and gentlemen. Just married and on honeymoon.

Remember Stan, now you're married you always get the last two words in: "Yes, dear."

'I knew a couple who went to Egypt for their honeymoon. She came back a mummy...'

Then the Sally Preston Dancers. A makeshift chorus line of girls plucked from factory dances and ballroom classes around North London.

During rehearsals she'd put the music on her portable wind-up gramophone and stand there with a cigarette drooping out the corner of her mouth while she drilled them in the finer points of sequence or whatever routine they were introducing to the show.

'Right ladies, en-pointe!

'Elsie I've seen better hair on a chimpanzee, sort yourself out by tonight dear...and Doris, for goodness sake, another ladder in your tights... are you hoping some burly fireman will climb up them?

'Okay, stop sniggering, Shelia and Dot, why don't you show us the Cha Cha Cha? And

one...two...three...'

Next up was Vince and the 'mysterious belle of the Orient' Suzie Wong, who did magic and knife throwing.

Vince had been in the circus before Dickie found him. Suzie may have dressed as a Chinese woman, but she was christened Agnes and was born in Dartmouth. Nothing a silk dress and a half hour with the make-up bag couldn't fix.

'Ah so Mr. Vince. Why you no saw women in half anymore?'
'Well Suzy, I got fed up with having so many half sisters.'

Sammy the Witch Doctor was first up after the interval. He was black as the ace of spades but sang with the voice of an angel. Dickie used to tell how he'd heard a beautiful voice singing as he walked past Pentonville prison, went in and found out it was Sammy, detained at his Majesty's pleasure after being caught selling his love potions.

He paid his fine and took him under his wing. He said a voice like that shouldn't be caged behind bars.

Utter poppycock of course, Sammy was really Walter Newton, a trained singer who came over from America fronting a dance band, fell in love and decided to stay. When love turned sour Dickie signed him up.

If a landlady refused to let Walter stay, Dickie would march the whole troupe out. We spent more than a few nights wandering around looking for digs, and one or two sleeping on station platforms.

Dickie used to say, *'I'm not having someone treating my darkie like a darkie.'*

One evening Kirk decided to resurrect his minstrel routine. Straw boater, banjo, black face, and huge white lips. I caught Walter watching from the wings.

'This Chinese couple had a baby and, thing was, the baby was black...so they called it Sum Ting Wong.'

Walter told me that back home in America he was fired from a showband and replaced with a white man who blacked his face with burnt cork. He left the show soon after that.

The dancers did a second set, ballroom stuff to start with but it became jazzier as fashions changed. Then Kirk did his big turn, a comic song, bit of patter with the audience and a bit of light opera, before he introduced the star act. That was Doreen and Alan Cartwright.

They had been in films where they often starred opposite each other. Their act was pure schmaltz. Light comedy, a tired tap dance routine, and stuff from their films that everyone knew and clapped, sang, or swooned along to.

The best bit of acting they did was to convince audiences that they were a happy couple. Offstage they loathed the sight of each other and stayed in separate rooms.

Alan tried to work his way through the chorus line. Sally would warn them about him when they joined and if she left any doubt in their star struck heads, Doreen made it quite plain to them that her husband's peccadillos would ruin their career.

Some nights we'd have a guest star. Dickie would call in a few favours. Will Hay even used me in his act. He played a schoolmaster, and I was a rather dim pupil.

'You silly boy...why have you got cotton wool in your ears?'

'Well, you keep saying that things go in one ear and out the other, so I am trying to keep them all in sir.'

Funny really. When I look back those days are like watching it all at the pictures. I remember them vividly, the smells of paint, turpentine and cigarettes backstage. The bottle of wine Kirk kept stage right, the dancers adjusting their straps and checking each other's lipstick. Suzie and Sally arguing over who the flowers addressed to *'My Sweet S'* were for. Dickie always promising a guest star when things were a getting a bit stale.

When Dickie wound it up, I went solo. He got me a few gigs and things went up from there. Life became a summer season in a boarding house doing end of the pier variety and winter I'd get some gigs around the city, in the nightclubs and variety shows, and get to spend the days with my ailing Ma.

My big break came when I toured with comedian and ventriloquist Peter Fraser and his puppet Bobby Baxter.

Bobby was an impish character, spiteful sometimes but being a puppet, he could get away with murder.

Peter was a real gent and tried to keep Bobby in his place. They were quite the double act, even if it was just one person.

'Hey Peter, how come that lady in the third row is so ugly?'

'That's no way to talk to a lady Bobby, apologise immediately.'

'Okay, hey misses, I'm sorry that you're so ugly.'

'Right, that's it, back in your case with you. I'm sorry madam, he's been a tad bilious lately, I'm afraid it might be woodworm.'

I really learnt the graft involved in life on the stage working with Peter and handling the pressure of always coming up with fresh material.

Peter was a seasoned performer; he'd put the work into a show for an old folks party or the children's ward at the hospital as much as he would for a two night full house at The palladium.

We did the wireless too and I'd voice a couple of characters on The Bobby Baxter show.

I eventually became a regular character. Bobby, well, Peter really, christened me the Chipper Chappie.

'Now it's over to Burton Coggles – the Chipper Chappie. Make them smile Burton...

'Hey Bobbie, you know all those books I gave you for Christmas?

'Well, they're due back at the library in a weeks time.'

The wireless was a new challenge. You had to keep coming up with new stuff, so Dickie put me in touch with a writer called Baz Butler.

Barry 'Baz' Butler.
Speeches, Jokes, Toasts.
Don't fret, Send SAE NOW
FREE samples.

That's what his card said.

He sent me a fortnightly letter full of them for three shillings plus a shilling for each one I used. Goodness knows where he got them, but we were a great team.

'Here, I'll tell you something, in the bar last night this chap comes up to me and he says "Burton", he says, "have a gander at this photograph. That's my fiancée that is, isn't she a stunner?"

'I had a look and I said, "If you think she's a stunner you should see my Maud."

'He said, "Why, is she a stunner too?"

'No, I said, she's an optician!'

Peter and I toured together. We became a couple, but it was hard in those days. When Dickie's secretary booked us in for a stint at some seaside boarding house for the summer, we always had separate rooms.

Some of the landladies were smart

though. When we arrived, a suitcase and a suit carrier each and an extra case with Bobby folded up inside, they'd ask us if we wanted to 'share a room to save a few bob?' That was the code.

If we said yes then they got to keep the rent Dickie sent for two rooms anyway and if they let the other room, they split the rent with us.

I invented my wife Maud for my act.

'Cor, isn't this weather foul. Since it started raining, all my Maud has done is look through the window...If it gets any worse, I'll have to let her in.

'No, no, no, that's mean of me. I take my Maud everywhere I go. Well, it saves me having to kiss her goodbye.

'Twice a week we go to a nice restaurant, have a little drinkie, good food and company. Maud goes on Tuesdays, and I go on Fridays.'

Things didn't last with Peter. He ended up marring a girl called Cindy from the chorus line. I was joint best man, along with that puppet.

'It's been an emotional day, even the cake is in tiers.

'What did you think of my speech

Bertie?'

'Well Bobby, I thought you were a bit wooden...Shall I take it from here?

'I don't believe in embarrassing the groom on his special day. Therefore, this speech won't contain anything uncomfortable or controversial about Peter. Instead, I'll refer only to the kind, funny side of his character. Thank you and goodnight.'

I know it's a cliché but I was really married to the job.

'Marriage is like a deck of cards. In the beginning all you need is two hearts and a diamond. By the end you wish you had a club and a spade.'

When war broke out again, I signed up to do forces entertainment. If Dickie had put me on stage and Peter had taught me the trade, then performing in front of crowds of rowdy servicemen really sharpened my act.

'Tommy was going home on leave by train. When it reached its first stop, a General walked in, and the soldier stood up. The General said, "At ease soldier, sit down."

'Anyway, the train reached the next

stop, so Tommy stands up again, and the General once again said, "At ease soldier, sit down."

'*When the train reached its third stop, Tommy springs up.*

'*This time, the General looked at him and said, "You don't have to salute every time we reach a stop."*

'*Tommy said, "Sir, I want to get off, I missed my stop two stations ago."'*

I did public information shorts on the wireless too and my 10 minutes of comedy and information became a bit of a cult.

'*Hello everyone in wireless land, Burton Coggles here, the Chipper Chappie making your dinnertime happy and your suspenders snappy.*

'*You know what listeners; old Adolf was sitting around the fire one evening petting his dog. Eva turns to him and says, "Hey Adolf, I think you love that dog more than you love me."*

So, Adolf turns to her and says "Well Eva, is it any surprise? When I go out and lock you both in the garage – he is the only one pleased to see me when I come home.

'*Hey, aren't the nights drawing in, winter draws on folks.*

Tell you what, you need to be careful

out there with the blackout. Here's my advice...
Burton's own blackout code
Is stay on the path and keep off the road.
Never step out to meet a bus,
Don't barge about or make a fuss,
Be a good-un and wait in line,
And you'll get home in plenty of time.'

Well, it worked at the time.

After the war it was harder to make a living, but I kept flogging my act. Pantomime became a winter staple for acts like mine struggling to survive until the summer holiday season.

That's when I became a Dame. Outrageous frocks, layers of slap on my face and a bucket full of sweets to throw at the audience.

Those forces shows really prepared me for the rough and tumble of a matinee full of sticky toddlers and grannies drunk on half a pint of milk stout.

'Hey Buttons, every time I'm down in the dumps, I buy myself a new hat.'
'I wondered where you got them from.'
'You cheeky so and so, that's it, I'm off for my bath in milk.'
'Pasteurised?'
'No, just up to here.'

Panto was a lifesaver. The cast became close as rehearsals turned to performances, the big name parachuted in to get bottoms on seats would have to muck in as much as the rest of us.

Two hours to get into costume for a five-minute publicity shoot with the local rag. Waltzing around the hospitals, sanitoriums and childrens homes, handing out sweeties and free tickets to the managers. Then when we'd all recovered from the end of season shindig summer season beckoned.

Together with a few wireless spots this became my year. And the year after that, and so on. One season merged into another. A bedsit with ice inside the windows in the winter and in the summer, a room overlooking the yard so that the good rooms could be let to holidaymakers.

I resisted the lure of the Cinema, the Pinewood Pound. The Hollywood Dollar.

That's a fib. I didn't resist it. Truth is, no one asked me. Little Arthur Askey, Will Hay, they all did it. Will even had his wife play the schoolboy part I'd done.

'Sir, was Joan of Arc Noah's wife?'
'You silly boy...'

As the seasons rolled into one, winter

Dame and summer Chipper Chappie, I began to get agitated and irritable if things changed, like new cast members who weren't quite up to the mark or a change of venue because sales weren't what the promoter expected.

One night, at the Cromer Pavilion I think it was, the chap on the stage door asked who I was. He was an old boy, just helping out for cigarette money.

Well, I exploded at him! How didn't he know who I was, I threatened to get him the sack.

It was like I was watching someone else throwing a tantrum. Then I went into my dressing room and broke down.

It cast a blanket over the night. Indifferent performances all round because the faded star, the act on the poster in a font slightly smaller than the headline, was such a prima donna.

I'd get annoyed if a changeover was tardy or if someone came in late for a performance. That used to be meat and bones to me. A perfect opportunity to sparkle, ask them who they were, where they were from, anything to play off and make good clean fun of.

'Blimey, are you late for the matinee or early for tonight? Does that shirt itch, because

it did when I gave it to the Red Cross'.

During the war people were regularly late, what with air raids, blackouts, transport disruption.

After the war it was hardly unusual. But that night it threw me more often than it should. I lost my rhythm and The Chipper Chappie became the Snappy Chappie, at least he did to the cast and crew.'

'I hope you're late because you stopped to make an appointment at the diet clinic love.

'Or were you in the cake shop?

'Look out gents, heavy load coming through, mind your toes...

'What's your name...any idea? Edna. We've all been waiting for you Edna.

'Comfy now? Taken the weight off your feet? It's the chair I feel sorry for...do you mind if we continue?'

I was a complete git.

My act was becoming stale too. I couldn't remember new material like I used to. Baz was still sending his typewritten pages but increasingly I didn't get the references or fought to recall the punchline so I kept reusing the old stuff that came easier to me.

My bookings were less and less

frequent. I was slipping down the bill and competition with the cinema and television meant audiences were down anyway.

'Two television aerials got married. The reception was fantastic!'

Summer season in Skegness. A half full matinee, most of those probably just looking for somewhere inside away from the rain.

I was fourth on the bill, still enough of a name to attract the older members of the family. Safe, clean, and trusted to send people into the interval with a smile on their face and their hands in their purses.

'Ladies and Gentlemen, please give a big Skegness welcome to the man who's guaranteed to put a smile on your face, the Chipper Chappie himself, Mr Burton Coggles!'

Out I went to applause, took my mark front and centre. Follow spot draws out and...

...and nothing. No idea why I was there or who these people were.

The lights hurt my eyes for the first time ever. I was totally bewildered. Rooted to the stage.

Applause turned to nervous laughter

and then to coughing.

Someone stage right prompted me to start. Then the compere, Lance Peters, appeared at my side, all matey and professional, he tried to make it seem like part of my act.

'Look at him, made of solid teak.' He put a hand on my back.

'Gottle of gear...' He said through tight lips, making me into his dummy. Bobby to his Peter.

'Allo Skegness...' He continued then pulled his hand away. I remember missing the warmth of his hand on the small of my back.

'He's only been doing this for 40 years. Tell you what Skegness, let's try another big round for the king of variety, the Chipper Chappie...'

While they clapped I turned to look at him. To this day I remember every detail of his face. The pores on his nose, the caking of the slap around his nostrils, the nicotine stain on his moustache, little rivers of broken capillaries on his cheeks, the way his right eyelid drooped a bit, Brylcreem melting on his temples. The smell of tobacco and whisky on his breath.

In that moment I loved him. He was my saviour. He looked into my eyes, and I let him lead me off to the sound of our footsteps.

As soon as we were in the wings, he shouts at the dancers to get on, sends a runner to the band to tell them to scrub me out and then asks me what happened.

He was angry of course, but he knew me well enough to know I wouldn't ruin the show, or my career, on purpose.

The next night he insisted on staying on when I was introduced. Made sure I was okay. Which was decent of him.

'Last night walking out here I fell through the floor. It was just a stage I was going through.

'My Maud was in the kitchen cooking bacon and eggs, when I heard a loud thud. I found her collapsed on the floor. Out for the count she was.

'Cor blimey I thought, I'm in a pickle now... then I remembered that Joe's Café does a lovely fry-up for a shilling!'

I was alright for a while, but it happened again. That terrifying emptiness. The sense that the familiar is just out of reach, an atom and a universe away at the same time.

In the butchers, at the launderette and one time I woke up on a park bench by the grandstand, no idea how I got there. I didn't tell anyone about these of course.

One evening I went back to my lodgings after a show and got in a terrible argument with the landlady's husband. Big chap with hairy arms hanging out of his grubby vest. Threw me out by the scruff of my neck.

It turned out I was staying somewhere else that year. Eventually I got back to the theatre and a stagehand walked me home.

The following evening, I was moved further down the bill, 'For your own good dear boy...you know, maybe you should see a doctor.'

I did. He told me it was my nerves, that I needed a wife, to take more fruit and asked if I had tried smoking?

'I went to the doctors yesterday and I asked him if he could give me something for my liver.

'He gave me half a pound of onions.

'I said, help me please Doc, I'm getting shorter and shorter!

'He said, "wait there and be a little patient!"'

Eventually they did some tests, over the winter while I was lodging in London. Dickie had retired by then but we kept in touch. His lungs were being eaten away by cancer and his son had taken over. He was a real sharp businessman. Very modern, he was all for television.

He said variety was dead. There was no money in it.

Well to be honest he was right. After the nurse had taken an armful of blood I sat in my room and it hit me. I'd worked from 14 years old. Been away when my Pa took his life, been away when my Ma eventually faded away from the TB.

I'd filled the Empires and Palladiums, the Palaces and Pavilions, from Glasgow to Portsmouth and now I was lodging over a Greengrocers in Tottenham.

Some days I forgot names or looked at familiar supermarkets as if they'd just landed from outer space, trying to remember if they'd always been there or were new.

Evenings I sobbed myself to sleep in the threadbare chair squeezed between the wardrobe and bed.

'I always sleep with a ruler, well when I wake up, I want to know how long I was asleep.

'I woke up with a puzzled look on my face. I had fallen asleep on my crossword.'

The morning after my test results, I took myself off for a walk. I knew what was happening. My mind was happier in the old days. The past and present kept colliding and the past was winning.

I'd noticed my dreams were all set when I was much younger. Faces long forgotten. Theatres I'd played in my teens, these were my nighttime refuges.

Familiar names of friends and shopkeepers danced on my tongue longing to be heard but tantalisingly out of reach. Often, I felt lost on my own streets, even when I knew every crack in the pavement. Come to think of it, I often felt lost in my own skin.

I wasn't ready for my second childhood. That's what one of the landladies had called it. She was looking after her husband, not much older than I was and away with the fairies. Followed her around like a lost puppy.

I didn't want that.

'If you cross a sheepdog with a jelly, do you get the collie wobbles?'

I wandered out of the West Green

Road, a hello and tip of the hat to the old man getting his nag ready for the rag and bone round. Another old timer on his way out. Once he packs it in there'd be no one to take his place.

I turned up the high road, past the posh three-story houses and the streets with piles of rubble like rotten teeth. They were pulling them down, making way for a new road and new homes.

Waiting for the die-hards to move out; or die.

There are so many people about now, scuttling around. I sat on a bench on the Green and wondered where they all came from, where they were going. They all seemed busy – preoccupied, heads down, hands in their coats or carrying umbrellas.

The women's clothes seemed to fit them better than they used to, and they had colours that gleamed, not washed out and drab. There were quite a few black faces around too. On the buses, in the shops. I wonder what Sammy, sorry, Walter would have made of it all. The shops selling fruits and veg I'd never seen before. Exotic stuff.

Everything has changed. Over night. I was only away for a while. A season or two. Maybe three.

I dodged a kid on a scooter. *'I was the Cheeky Cherub when I was your age,'* I called after him.

'Whatever you say grandad!'

The Regal had seen better days. I played there a few times.

'I took my Maud to watch a film at the Regal.

'A few minutes after it started, I heard her rustling around and searching on the floor. "What are you doing?" I asked her.

'I had a toffee in my mouth and it dropped out.'

'Just leave it, it'll be filthy now. There's plenty more in the bag.

'But I've got to find it Burton," she said, "my teeth are still in it!'

It's all noise now. Hustle and bustle, cars, bicycles, lorries, buses pulling in and out, taxi cabs honking at them and trains rattling by overhead and underground. And people. People everywhere.

I used to live around here. There have been so many anonymous rooms I've called home. Neat and damp. Ha! Sounds like a double act from the golden days.

'Hey Neat, why do cows have bells?

'I don't know Damp, why do cows have bells?'

'Because their horns don't work...'

'Hey Neat, did you know I used to run a lonely hearts service for chickens?'

'No, I didn't know that Damp. Why did you give it up?'

'I couldn't make hens meet.'

There was a chap with a big barrow full of vegetables coming up the path, so I stepped into the road to avoid him.

'Today was a terrible day. My Maud got hit by a bus...

'To make it worse I lost my job as a bus driver.'

I woke up in hospital. Clean sheets, pretty nurses, and an old boy opposite emptying his lungs into a kidney bowl.

Nothing serious they told me. A few bruises, nothing broken. The doctor said I was lucky, then he asked me who the Prime Minister was.

Silly old fool, like I wouldn't know that. Couldn't recall the name right then and there. Atlee? No that didn't sound right.

They told me I'd got upset and shouted at them so they gave me something to calm my nerves.

'The doctor asked me if I'd taken my medicine?

'I said no, you told me to drink it after my bath, but after I drank my bath, I didn't have room for the medicine.'

I had a dream about Peter. I remembered how he always used to cover Bobby's eyes with a spotted hanky when we went to bed. His shaving mirror propped against his suitcase, the scrapbook of press cuttings he carried everywhere. His suit and tie hanging on the back of the door. The way he smelled, woody and spicy, like fresh pipe tobacco.

We lost touch after the wedding. I heard his wife left him after a year or so. Scarpered one night and never seen again.

Probably glad to get away from him and that cursed puppet. I'd bump into him occasionally on the circuit, he was polite, but I heard he used my name in his act as a by-word for old fashioned out of touch performers. Odd that.

Next thing I remember is a nurse taking a tray away from me. She asked me if I'd enjoyed my bangers and mash. I suppose I must have; my plate was clear.

'Never throw food away Bertie, there's little black babies in Africa starving.' That's what my Ma always told me. I wonder if she'll come and visit me?

'I was sitting down to supper with my Maud the other day. I said, here, pass me another slice of gravy love...well, I'm not saying she can't cook, but we had burnt salad for our supper.'

Water works. That's what it was. An infection 'down below'. But then they said something about needing care.

This Indian doctor told me my mind was wandering. He asked me if I had blackouts? Were there days that I couldn't remember? Did I know who was on the Throne?

I said *'No, but when we hear a flush, we can look to see who comes out...'*

I don't think he understood.

After a few days they sent me to some new place with a bag of pills and a new coat. I kept asking them when I'm going home but they never gave me a straight answer. They said I would be here a while and not to worry.

'Just settle in Mr. Coggles and let the nurses take care of you.'

Now I'm in this place that smells of bleach and wee. It's too warm and the air is stale, plays havoc with my voice. I told them I need fresh air; my voice is my career and I must look after it. They are very polite but I don't think they really listen.

There are high backed chairs around the wall of the lounge. A bookcase with stacks of large print books that no one reads, a big radiogram with the wireless tuned to something loud all the time. 'Popular' music they call it.

I told the nurse that I used to be on the wireless.

'Of course you were Bertie,' she said.

Maybe they can get me back on. When I'm better.

Minnie, moaning Minnie I call her, keeps wandering about the place talking to herself. Her son comes in lunch times to see her. When Minnie sits down, she rocks back and forth picking at her sleeve for a minute or two then wanders off.

I see the sadness in her sons' eyes as he makes pleasant with the rest of us, asking how we are? He told me he works as a teller in the bank and pops in at lunchtime to see his mother.

'I lost my job at the bank on my very first day, a woman asked me to check her balance, so I pushed her over.'

Some other old dear, Elsie I think, keeps complaining that she's in the workhouse and wants to go home. Some of the others don't say anything, just sit there until they fall asleep, mouths hanging open, dribbling into their laps.

Tough crowd.

A bloke over the way told me to eff off because I was sitting in his chair!

Rough old geezer, hands like saucers with sausages hanging off. Not a hair left on his head and arms like a gorilla. Bet he was a bit tasty back in the day, could look after himself.

Anyway, just as I was getting comfy in another chair, he started up again.

'Ere, I know you. No, no, no, don't tell me, it'll come to me...'

I left him to it. Silly old sod.

'Here Nurse, I got sick after drinking that cream. My stomach was churning for a while, but now I'm feeling butter.'

Then the old coot in the chair pipes up. 'That's it! Coggles. As I live and breathe the Cheeky ... no, the Chipper Chappie. It is you, isn't it? '

I confirmed I was, I am, Burton Coggles. Turns out he'd seen me a few times. He used to drive buses for a living and got into the shows for free when he brought a bus load in.

'I got to thinking about my life and all the people I've lost....maybe I shouldn't have been a tour guide after all.'

Long story short, he turns into my best pal and even organised a wireless show for me. Well sort of, it was onto a tape. I thought I'd be in a studio with a reel to reel but they just set up a microphone and a small box on a wobbly table overlooking the garden. Even so it was wonderful to be back on the airwaves and it was so simple to operate.

Lionel, that's his name, he brought some of his gramophone collection into the lounge and played tunes between my links and jokes.

It was a bit ropey, there were a lot of gaps and the volume was a bit iffy. I told him to stop fiddling with his knob at one point and we both lost it. Completely corpsed, live on air, I was sobbing with laughter, more so when he then played a record at the wrong speed.

'Cor blimey Lionel, that record was faster than your toupee in a hurricane.

'That Lionel, he gave me a little wireless with no batteries. I think it's a wind up.

'I asked him where he gets his love of music from, he said his father was a conductor

– he always listened to the radio on his bus.'

We ended up re-recording the whole show. I hadn't laughed like that in years. Better therapy than any of the nonsense they try here or the pills I'm popping.

Nurse Alan arranged to have it played it over the tannoy in the home on Christmas day.

'Greetings everyone out there in wireless land, Burton Coggles here, the Chipper Chappie. A very merry Christmas to you all. I'm joined by Mr. Music himself Lionel 'the ladies man' Wilson. Say hello to the listeners Lionel.

'Hello to the listeners Lionel.'

'You silly sausage. Tell you what, isn't the wireless wonderful. I saw one for sale for £5 with a broken volume control. Well, I couldn't turn it down.

What's your first record Lionel?'

'White Christmas by Bing Crosby.'

'Wonderful! You know that Bing Crosby wasn't always a good boy. Once he stole an advent calendar and got 25 days.'

I still get forgetful. Days seem to pass that I can't recall. I must have done something, been somewhere. I must have eaten. Sometimes I nod off after lunch and wake up in the theatre.

The buzz of the audience shuffling along the aisles, the wave of people as they stand to let others through. The conductor rifling through sheets of music, reminding the band that they've changed the running order. The stagehands milling around, checking their cues on a typed sheet pinned behind the backdrop. The clang as the handle for the curtains is unlocked, the dancers costumes dull and lifeless out of the spotlight. The smells of pipe tobacco, grease paint and sawdust. Rocking on the balls of my feet as the announcer taps the microphone. The boy frantically waving to the conductor to start the intro music, the curtain twitching, the way silence spreads through the auditorium, the squeak of my shoes as I step out 'always have a hanky and shiny shoes son,' the spotlight warming my face, a nod to the conductor, arms spread to soak up the applause, then a modest damping down gesture to the stalls...

'Good evening Ladies and Gentlemen, what a wonderful reception...It's an absolute pleasure to be here.

'On the way to the show I bought a pencil with two erasers. Don't know why, it's pointless...'

Sometimes I wish I didn't have to wake up.

For a while I don't know if I'm there or here. Then the smell of cabbage and air freshener reminds me those days are no more. Not like that.

But I still have Tuesday afternoons. That's when Lionel and I record our show. After a while they started copying the tapes and sending them to other homes. We even got fan mail.

'We've had a letter from Doris in Neasden. She's in hospital because some books fell on her...well Doris, you've only got your shelf to blame.'
'What's up next Lionel?
'Lionel?
'Lionel, are you okay?'

He wasn't okay. His heart gave out, just like that.

At his funeral his daughter gave me a hug and said he'd gone doing what he loved. His record collection was his pride and joy. He'd always come back from a week driving the old dears around the sights with a long new player or two tucked under his arm.

'Do you know the last thing he said to

me before he kicked the bucket? "Burton, watch how far I can kick this bucket."'

I lost the will to go on after that. Alan tried to get me set up again, but nothing came of it. The Chipper Chappie had left the building.

After all, what did I ever do? Tell some jokes, helped holiday makers pass the time between bingo and a cheeky sherry before bed, or put a frock on to keep families occupied for a couple of hours during the bleak mid-winter.

I'm not bitter, not really. I had good times. Apart from Peter they were mostly on the stage or in a shabby studio though.

The rest, well it was trains and bedsits and notebooks full of jokes. Chewed pencils and crossed out punchlines. Suspicious landladies and too-big-for-their-boots co-stars, bored musicians, threadbare tuxedos, and lonely walks home through darkened streets.

You'd done your turn, made them smile, now just scuttle back to the darkness until it's time to do it all again.

But when they're shrieking with laughter, when even the crew are smiling, they're whistling and whooping in the stalls, the band seem reluctant to take up their instruments for your big finish, when you don't notice the spot in your eyes, when it flows like mercury and you've got them in the palm of your hand and could go on all night, then it was all worthwhile...

'I'm wondering about getting a glass coffin...remains to be seen.'

Sometimes I wish I didn't have to wake up.

'Thank you, ladies and gentlemen. Goodnight!'

Ray Canham

The Coffee Hut

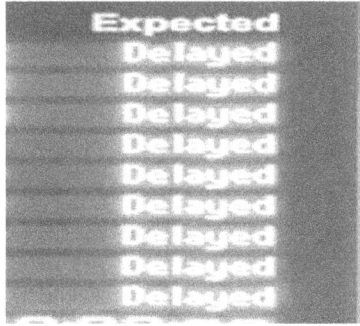

She caught my attention by waving enthusiastically towards the station concourse below. We were on the balcony overlooking the departures board.

I was waiting for my Americano at the coffee bar, my train was delayed because someone jumped from a bridge onto the tracks. She was seated alone at a tiny table squeezed between the coffee hut and the glass wall of the balcony.

She was elderly, thin with deep blue veins standing out from bony white hands. Her hair was bright white and thinning but she had taken time to set it in loose curls. Her face was powdered with rouge cheeks and ruby lips.

She waved again, pointed to her teacup and a broad smile broke across her face. I assumed she'd caught the attention of the person she was there to meet.

I took my coffee and wandered to the bookshop to get something to read while I waited for my train.

A week later I went back to the same place for coffee and there she was, resplendent in a powder blue coat with a dripping umbrella leant against the glass wall. I nodded to her, and she smiled back then immediately looked back towards the concourse below, scanning the tide of passengers disembarking from their trains.

After three more weeks we'd become nodding acquaintances and I ventured a 'hello', which she responded to with a demure 'good morning'.

The following week my regular Tuesday meeting at the Woking office was changed to Wednesday, so I wasn't surprised that she wasn't there.

I asked Emily, who was making my coffee, if the woman was there every week. 'The old girl? Yes, every Tuesday, she's off her rocker if you ask me, but harmless enough, not like some we get here'.

'She seems nice, just waiting for her visitor I suppose,' I said.

'Nah, she just sits there all morning nursing a cup of tea, then scuttles out, never meets anyone as far as I can see, just a sad old lady. Sugar?'

'Eh? Oh, no thanks. She sounds lonely.'

'Probably,' she said moving on to the next customer. All week I had the image of her in my head, and I wondered who she was waiting for. Maybe it was a relative, a favoured niece perhaps who popped in to keep an eye on her, or a son, daughter, even husband; although I doubted this last scenario one never knew for sure. Well, not unless I asked her which seemed nosey, it wasn't any of my business after all.

The following week I took my coffee, nodded to her, and took up position leaning against a pillar at a point below the departure board.

After a few minutes I saw a young lady on the concourse wave in her direction and quicken her pace, her case clattering around erratically as she dragged it behind her. I smiled to myself and looked back towards the old lady.

Who wasn't there. I expected to see her on the escalator but on turning back I saw the young lady in the arms of a man of about her age.

Dammit, I thought, as I rushed to catch my train.

On my next visit to the station, I was wrestling with the lid of my coffee cup when a brittle voice said, 'they are awkward aren't they, I always have a proper cup.'

'Yes, they are', I said, as scalding coffee spilled down the sides of the flimsy cup.

'Would you like to sit down and enjoy it properly? Everyone is in such a rush and proper tea, or coffee, should be enjoyed, not gulped down while running for a train,' she said.

'That's very kind, I'd love to, I said, 'but I have a train to catch, I've a meeting soon.'

'That's a shame, I'm Gwen by the way.'

'Oh, er…Stephen, pleased to meet you, Gwen.'

'You too Stephen. I've seen you here before, haven't I?'

'Yes, my regular Tuesday meeting in sunny Woking.'

'That must be important to take you out there by train every week.'

'Well…' I thought about the team meetings; the Director reading out last week's sales figures we already knew, Emma from the Chelmsford branch moaning about the traffic, Peter and Mary raising the same issues that no one cared about and then using the opportunity to pick up stationery and free fruit from the staff room.

'Do you know what Gwen, it's really not important at all, just an opportunity to sit around and not do any real work.'

'So, nothing will go wrong if you're not there? The markets won't crash, or traffic come to a standstill?'

I smiled. 'No, do you know what Gwen, the only thing that would change if the meeting didn't take place would be a slight increase in our productivity.'

'Well, that's settled then, do sit down.'

I did as bid. For some reason I didn't feel like asking her about who she was waiting for just then.

After a few minutes of small talk about offices, I realised she hadn't looked away at the destination board or towards the passengers arriving in their droves below.

'Won't you miss your visitor?' I asked her.

Gwen looked away; a distant look crossed her face as she turned back to meet my gaze with piercing milky white eyes.

'Oh no, I don't think so dear.'

'That's good. Who are you waiting to meet? I said, adding, 'If you don't mind me asking that is?'

'That's a very good question Stephen, but rather hard to answer. I don't know, but I'll recognise them when I see them.'

I couldn't think of a suitable reply. Maybe Emily who made my coffee was right, perhaps she was just a lonely old lady living in the past.

I was busy rearranging my next question in my head to cause as little offence as possible when the background noise around us became subdued and muffled, like I was hearing everything through the thin walls of my old student flat.

Gwen was sipping her tea, apparently unaffected by the strange change in sound. Catching me looking at her she smiled and tilted her cup towards me before taking another sip.

I yawned, trying to unblock my ears as one would on an airplane, but sounds were still muffled. As I went to say something Gwen gently placed a bony white hand across mine.

'Don't fight it Stephen, everything's fine, relax. You'll feel better soon.'

'I'm sorry' I said, 'I feel a bit odd...'

'I know you do. It'll be okay. Stephen, can you hear me? Just nod if you can.'

I nodded as she'd asked. My head felt like it was in a vice, colours faded, my vision blurred.

'Just sit still, it's nearly over, just a few more seconds and ... there we are. Well done Stephen.'

The jolt was like waking from a bad dream, colour and sound rushed in, more quickly than my head could cope with, my left arm jerked and sent my cup flying off the table, the remains of my coffee spilling across the table and floor.

'Whoops a daisy' said Gwen, mopping it up with a napkin. 'At least you didn't soil yourself.'

'Eh?'

'At least you didn't soil...you haven't, have you? I don't mind but it's embarrassing for everyone when that happens.'

'Er no, I haven't.' I said, shaking my head to try and clear it. 'Sorry Gwen, I had an odd turn there, I'm not sure what happened.'

'Hmmm, I don't have time to explain now Stephen, I have work to do, oh look, here they come now. Five if I'm not mistaken, one little one this time, poor wee mite.' With that she waved in her familiar style and raised her teacup in the direction of the hall below.

Following her gaze, I felt a dense silence like the calm before a storm, which suddenly burst into noisy commotion. Staff ran towards the platforms, people were taking to their phones, scrolling madly, or holding them to their ears. Others stood looking at the departures board, where most of the trains were ticking over to 'delayed'.

I turned to Gwen, but she was gone. The staff and customers of the coffee hut were animated and talking excitedly so I got up to join the huddle and try and find out what was going on.

I looked around, watching the panic unfold below. A mop of bright white hair caught my eye, and I thought I saw an elderly lady carrying a toddler leading a small group through the ticket hall towards the exit. Then my phone burst into life with a succession of pings and alerts.

Dammit, the meeting, 'I'll have to think of an excuse for not being there' I thought while desperately trying to get the phone to recognise my fingerprint. When it eventually let me in, I had a missed call from the office, a couple of texts from colleagues and a breaking news alert, which I opened first.

'Reports are coming in that the 11.05 London Waterloo to Southampton train has derailed near Woking in Surrey.

Initial reports suggest at least five fatalities including one infant, and dozens of injuries. Emergency services on the scene. Further details to follow.'

The Weight of Sin

The Stirk

STIRK, *n., v. Also stirc, sturk, stirrock; and met. forms strick, strik(k) (I.Sc.). Dim. stirkie, -y.[stɪrk; I.Sc. strɪk]*

1. A young bovine animal after weaning, kept for slaughter at the age of two or three, not for breeding.

2. A sturdy young man.

3. A stupid, oafish fellow.

There is a legend told on the island about a 14th century Clan Chief who proved his fitness to rule without drawing his sword by a single feat of endurance.

He swam through an area notorious for strong and unpredictable currents to a small rock in the channel between the mainland and the island. He was the first person on record to swim to it.

The small, rocky isle looks, from some angles, a little like a bull and is known locally as the Stirk.

***

Simon swam out further into the sea. It was still cold, even though he had been in a few minutes. He felt his muscles working, concentrated on his breathing and kept half an eye open for jellyfish.

He reached the point of jagged rocks, which everyone knew marked the boundary for how far to swim in the bay. Beyond the currents became strong and unpredictable, with reefs hiding under the waters.

The sea was getting choppy without the shelter of the bay. He swapped from a lazy crawl to breaststroke, keeping his head up but still some waves washed over him and he'd surface with stinging eyes and bob around to get his bearings before setting off again.

With the waves he couldn't see any of the pale moon jellyfish until they were almost on him, several times he dived under to avoid them at the last minute. The cold water would help with the pain, but he knew from experience that he would feel it later.

If there was to be a later.

**

Swimming out to the island was forbidden. Everyone knew that. Parents warned children long before they could be trusted to paddle.

Teenagers were cautioned about the perils of smoking, strong liquor, and swimming to the Stirk. Only the latter was enforced with enthusiasm by adults.

Young men were occasionally goaded into trying but by the time a crowd of spectators had gathered someone had the sense to talk them out of it or to call somebody in authority to put a stop to it.

Today was Simon's second attempt. His first was when he was 19 years old. Tall and wiry with muscles honed by labouring in his father's small quarry, he had set off at low tide and had made it look easy.

For a while he was a local hero, at least to those of his age or thereabouts. As the boat that picked him up smacked against the stone of the jetty a small crowd cheered him ashore where he found himself the centre of a competing group of local girls.

***

The waves were growing as he trod water for a rest, he could feel the icy undercurrent dragging at his legs. He took a deep breath and plunged on. The Stirk didn't look any closer, but he was sure that he was over halfway so the tide should be turning, making it the safest and shortest distance to cross.

A mat of kelp floating by startled him, resulting in a mouthful of seawater, which he spat out just as a wave caught him. He flailed as he went under again and realised he was beginning to panic. He forced himself to let the water surround him, let himself sink a bit, release his remaining breath, and follow the bubbles to the surface.

He allowed himself to roll with the waves and get some air. The salty water stung his eyes, and he could feel himself weaker now as he trod water. He was about to settle into a slow crawl when he realised that the Stirk was behind him. He cursed his panic and lack of awareness.

It hadn't been this hard before.

Then, 45 years ago, he'd been sure of so much. He would be the first of his generation to swim to the Stirk. He'd have his pick of the local girls before going off to the mainland, maybe Glasgow with its grimy underbelly or Edinburgh, full of faded grandeur.

Wherever he went it would be away.

Not that he had much choice in the end. After he had made it to The Stirk word got around quickly on the small island community.

One or two other boys swore that they'd done the swim too, but an absence of witnesses meant no one believed them.

As he turned twenty years old in the arms of Jinny MacLeod, in a caravan behind the bus station, Gregory's body was found by a local fisherman on the rocks of Aulison point.

***

In the choppy waters Simon bobbed over a wave and sighted the Stirk, adjusted his course and set off.

Progress was wearying and slow, the waves were smaller now but relentless and hitting him at 45 degrees. He took regular mouthfuls of water, his eyes smarted and more than once he'd instinctively wiped them with the back of his hand and rubbed more salt in.

The cold that had gripped him as he swam through the calmer waters of the bay had settled into numbness, but he ploughed on, moving out of instinct. He knew that to stop for longer than to get his bearing could be fatal now. He was too numb to shiver, too cold to think clearly and too far out to turn back.

His mind wandered as he made slow strokes through the waters.

***

It had soon been understood that Gregory had tried the swim to the Stirk. A couple of his friends were already on their way over to it in a dinghy. They had kept clear of the swimmer so that the wash from their boat didn't hamper his progress but lost sight of him before they were halfway.

At the brief inquest that followed it turned out that they'd waited for him off the rocky shores of the Stirk for nearly an hour, then zig zagged back along what they hoped was the route, becoming increasingly worried as their tiny boat with an underpowered outboard motor struggled against the tide and currents.

Gregory was 18 when he was found on those rocks. At his funeral Simon listened to his short life condensed into a few sentences.

Second prize at the agricultural show for his bantams. A collection of mediocre school achievements and a few nice words...he was 'a popular lad with a winning smile. Always eager to help;' if you believed the carefully modulated words of his head teacher. Simon suspected he could not have picked Gregory out of a line up even if they all wore name badges. Scant reward for 18 years.

The thought had made him snort, and the whole bleak graveside assembly had looked his way as he tried to turn it into a cough. Maybe that's when it started?

Or was it when, after the service Gregory's mother, red eyed and bewildered, had pushed through her sisters, who orbited like fussy satellites, strode up to him and said that Gregory did what he did, and he wasn't a wee lad anymore so Simon should stop blaming himself for her son's death. Gripping his hand in both of hers, she squeezed tight for a few seconds then left him standing there, as she was engulfed by her family.

He hadn't blamed himself. Until that moment.

Gregory was an also ran at school, a nice enough boy who coasted along, kept bantams out the back of his parent's cottage and was so anonymous and overlooked that he had felt the need to prove himself by copying Simon's feat.

He wasn't a wee one to be minded. He was about to leave school, had a college course arranged, something technical, to do with electronics as far as Simon could recall. He may not have been the alpha male, but he wasn't picked on or bullied much either.

His family were decent enough folk. His mother helped the slower learners with reading sometimes and had always said hello to Simon in the corridor as she passed.

His father was an engineer, Simon wasn't sure what kind, but he was always out doing odd jobs for people, often down at the harbour fixing the engines of the small fishing boats, nursing them far beyond their natural life and probably in return for nothing more than a lobster or a couple of pints.

***

Simon was caught sideways by another wave, he spread out, face down in the water and let himself bob up, where he twisted over and floated, staring through eyes raw and half closed with salt. He watched the clouds move slowly across the sky, gentle, soft, and warm and he let himself sink into them, felt their warmth close around him...

***

A few months after the funeral he had left the island.

People had still said hello, he was served in the shops and pubs with politeness but there was little chatter, the gossip that was a constant undercurrent on the island bypassed him.

Some of the warmth had gone out of these everyday exchanges and he started to realise that he was the subject of gossip now. The boy who had foolishly swum to the Stirk and made every eager young buck on the island want to be him, to emulate their hero.

When two 14-year-old boys were pulled pale and shivering from the water that summer the icy politeness started turning to resentfulness, people avoided eye contact and he always seemed to be the last to be served in the pub.

***

A splash of foamy water hit him full in the face and he came to with a start, swallowing some seawater as he panicked and fought to tread water.

The waves on the surface were breaking now, white foam and spray whipped up by the wind. He heard the low chug of the ferry and looked around to see it disappearing around the end of the bay.

The wash would arrive soon, sending a swell his way that would break against the waves. He knew all he could do was ride it out...wait for the irregular rhythms to stop and the swell to die down before continuing.

He felt the cold now, too much time spent floating or treading water. He shivered knowing his only hope was to plough on, to move and to keep moving. As the wash from the ferry brought a wave to him, he rode it and tried to sight the Stirk but all he could see was the shores of the mainland in one direction and as he turned and rode the second wave, he could see the island behind him.

No Stirk.

***

No Stirk.

That had been the only time he had even thought of worrying last time when he couldn't see it. Then he had just trod water and got his bearings.

The current had carried him further into the channel than he had expected, so he had altered direction and in no time was scrambling over rocks draped with slippery kelp to await the boat he'd arranged to collect him.

Then the cuts on his knees and arms from the sharp rocky climb up only added to his heroic appearance and he recalled now how he had picked at them to make sure they ran with blood as he got out of the boat in front of his friends.

Still no Stirk.

Even treading water was an effort now. His legs were leaden and as he swam on, towards the far shore in what he hoped was the right direction, his feet barely broke the surface. His arms ached, his eyes were swollen, movement now out of habit, fearing if he stopped, his limbs would seize up altogether.

Last time he had energy to spare. His arms had ached a little, but he had felt like he could go on and on, on to the mainland even.

That was so long ago now though. Long before he had left to take his degree and drop out after the second year. He'd only taken it because he wanted, needed, to get away and the psychology degree course was about all he could get accepted on at the last minute.

After dropping out he'd drifted into bar work, initially to earn some spare cash, but full-time work was tempting and nothing he could learn in the lecture halls could prepare him for the customers of Glasgow's city centre bars.

With two thirds of a degree, as he liked to say, and a couple of years full time behind the bar of the Empress, he took on the job of managing it.

The next twelve years he saw it through good and lean times. He was fit, healthy, handsome; and an alcoholic.

His room above the Empress was barely bigger than the single bed it contained; a wardrobe held together with gaffer tape stood on a threadbare carpet in the corridor outside. The bathroom was a shower cubicle with a curtain that had fallen so many times he didn't bother with it anymore.

His world.

Sleep, clean, serve, sleep.

Helped along with alcohol and bad food from the café next door or a packet of crisps and a sandwich from the supermarket. That was his life for six days a week. Week in- week out, every day, except Tuesdays.

Tuesday was his day off and after a quick shopping run for the essentials he'd take himself off to the pool, where he kept up lengths until the chlorine closed his eyes and his muscles throbbed.

Tuesdays he was alcohol free and as he swam in an easy, lazy-looking crawl he imagined the weeks' worth of whisky floating out behind, a thick and greasy amber film following him as he tried to outswim his past and his demons.

He'd take a soup or baked potato in the café next door, gulp down a soft drink and return to his room to work through the orders and receipts until he slipped off to sleep, waking in the gloom of the late afternoon, surrounded by half-finished notes, columns of figures with obscure footnotes and reminders that he'd written to himself.

***

He could see the Stirk now. A few

strokes in and he rode the waves like a pro, felt some energy enter his body. He sighted on the distant rocks and switched to a crawl, settling into the rhythm of the sea, the swell and white caps pushed to the back of his mind.

He was in charge, one, two, three strokes, head up and breathe-in, to the left; four, five, six, head up to the right; breathe-out, repeat. Keep going, the pain was just in his head, arms and legs pumping away automatically.

One, two, three, breathe-in. He could taste the chlorine. If he squinted, he was able to sight the lane markers on the bottom, through the cool, clear water...four, five, six, head out and breathe in...no... out... exhale...exhale...

***

After one Tuesday swim, with a bundle of crumpled receipts logged into his notebook, he realised he had the rest of the week to himself.

The brewery was doing some renovations so the Empress would be closed for a few days. The area manager, a dour lady with a voice made harsh by years of smoking had insisted he take some of the holiday he was owed.

He had no one to go on holiday with, no friends beyond the regulars who propped up the bar and they might not even return if they found another snug while the Empress was closed.

He hadn't kept in touch with anyone from the island and his few friends from his university days were all scattered around the country and settled into careers and marriages.

On the odd occasion he had visited one of them he felt uncomfortable as they discussed mortgage rates and school catchment areas. All he could contribute was tales of drunks and brawlers or memories of his island upbringing as he eyed the bottle of wine on the table wondering if he could top his glass up even though everyone else's was still half full.

Every visit had reminded him his life was stalled and he was marking time until his turn came to sit on the other side of the bar, joylessly knocking back cheap blends with sullen men.

He decided to return to the island. He knew it was to say goodbye, although he never really acknowledged it. He just knew that a life of alcoholic oblivion wasn't an option, and yet neither was living on the island that had rejected him.

If he was bitter about it, he buried it

deep down under layers of cheap whisky and memories that were being eaten away by alcohol.

Sunday morning, out alone before the house woke up, he'd walked to the bay to shake off he fug of a late session with his dad. Older and greyer than last time he'd visited, the old man was pale and listless, fussed over by Simon's mum, who just kept going and never seemed to change.

Father and son had sat around sipping their drams into the wee hours. Strong silent men with a lifetime of emotions dammed behind whisky stained eyes.

The sun was up, gannets dived into the bay. The light caught the Stirk out at sea. Next thing Simon remembered he was lunging forward into the cold water.

***

Clear water now, filtered sunlight dancing on the crests of the waves. Other swimmers coming the other way, cutting the water with a dozen different strokes. Keeping to their lanes. Seaweed in the pool...that shouldn't happen.

Cold water, colder now than it should be. Switch to breaststroke, swim down into the cool dark water.

Down…

He erupted from the depths screaming with a voice so hoarse almost no sound came out. Flapping at his leg, he went back under and sprung up spitting out water.

He could almost taste the sting. Needle sharp and biting pain, spreading up his calf.

Between gasps he coughed up the salty water and dry heaved, treading water, going under again as a wave broke across him. His leg felt numb where the jellyfish had stung him, but the pain was inside now, nausea welling up as he fought to keep his head above water.

He could have cried. For the first time he felt despair. Until now he had been angry. Furious with the injustice of it all. Of the rejection, with the pub regulars who mirrored his decline, with Gregory for trying something he wasn't capable of. Angry with his parents for their mute acceptance that going away was probably for the best. Angry with his missed opportunities, angry with everything that had happened that he couldn't change, and angrier still with the things he could have changed but hadn't.

He kept the anger inside. Pent up and suppressed like a coiled spring. It found ways to sneak out in sarcastic comments, arguments with customers, a little too much force to eject a drunk at closing time.

And the drink kept it down, stopped him from having to think too much.

Damn, his leg hurt. He could still kick with it as he swam on, but he felt every stroke in the tendons, the welt he knew was forming was like needles injecting him with fire. He could see more jellyfish now, drifting with the tide. Big purple ones like floating brains in aspic, trailing the poison in their long tentacles.

He was coasting along, floating with the barest of strokes, delirious and spent. He had no energy; the pain of the sting had sapped the last of his fight. His eyes were swollen and his vision blurry, he couldn't see the Stirk, but then he could barely see his own hands.

He rolled over onto his back and let the waves wash him. The sun was warm and he felt a peace of sorts. His leg hurt, his eyes were swollen and raw, every muscle ached, he was thirsty and hollow inside, the salt tightened his skin as the sun dried it but there was a calmness too. The tide was turning, and the waters were calmer.

This is it, he thought. He surprised himself that he felt no panic or alarm. He'd wanted to prove himself again, to recreate that moment that changed everything. One last do-or-die push for glory. He knew he'd be found eventually, maybe on the same rocks where they found Gregory's body.

This was better than fading away on a greasy bar stool and drifting into oblivion in a boozy stupor, or if he was unlucky strapped to a bed as he went cold turkey in a sterile hospital ward, no drink except tepid tea from a beaker, and visitors who couldn't find the right words to say, worrying about overstaying their parking permit and shuffling off to lunch in the pub over the road.

Seabirds wheeled overhead, the sun was warm, the sea calm. He let his feet sink and spread his arms.

I'm ready, he thought.

His foot touched rock...

The Weight of Sin

Ray Canham

The Man Who
Spoke To No One

He spoke to no one.

Rude they said. A miser, a misery, a grumpy old man.

His neighbours were out at work all day. They spent their evenings in the glow of their television sets.

At weekends they shopped or ran children to clubs and parties.

His post, what little he received, arrived before he got up. If there was a delivery for next door, they rang his doorbell and left the package on his doorstep.

Next door would collect them without disturbing him.

He would go to the shop once a week. The man on the till didn't bother to disguise his impatience while he packed his tins into a plastic bag. The people waiting in the queue would tut.

His daughter used to call him on Sunday afternoons but now she'd hang up if he took his time getting out of his chair. She seldom answered when he called her.

She had set up direct debits for most of his bills. Occasionally he received letters in brown envelopes and sent cheques off in return.

He sent birthday and Christmas cards with ten-pound notes inside to his grandchildren. They would send a thank-you by text to the mobile phone he could not use.

He tapped his card on a machine on the bus for his ticket to town. The driver sat behind a Perspex screen and barely acknowledged him.

The library was automated. Sometimes he would deliberately scan the same book twice just so that someone would have to come and assist him. A fleeting exchange of human contact.

He used to go to the bank, but one day a lady showed him how to use the card he hadn't asked for in the machine in the lobby and implied that he wouldn't be welcome at the window with his old fashion cheque book.

The council wrote to him about using Apps, QR codes and 'doing it online.'

His doctors had an automated phone system that he couldn't navigate and he had no idea what a hash button was that would have connected him to a real person.

The minutes of the day stretched into hours measured by the ticking of the clock in the hall. Days became weeks, became months.

His phone stopped ringing, the door stayed closed, the pantry wasn't restocked.

When he was found, they asked why he didn't talk to anyone.

Ray Canham

Whitehall

He had no idea where he was. He'd been picked up in a police raid and put in a cell. It wasn't unpleasant by the standards of some he'd been in.

The police were polite and the questioning benign, almost friendly. No one tried to accuse him of anything except living above a brothel. They didn't even raise the age of the girls, which he would have denied any knowledge of anyway. He had been confident that he had destroyed anything incriminating when the commotion began downstairs.

Then a few hours ago he'd been taken to what he assumed was more questioning, but instead had been handcuffed, hooded, and led by persons unknown into a van. After that he lost track of time, but he estimated it was about two hours later when he was led still hooded and handcuffed to a new cell.

***

Michael approached the building with a mixture of trepidation and excitement. He'd been contacted to do some private work for the government by an email to his personal account, which was swiftly followed by a low-key meeting in a coffee shop, and a follow-up email with instructions to report to an address in Whitehall.

He paused, took a deep breath and opened the door. Inside, his invitation and ID were checked, and he was directed through a metal detector to an uncomfortable sofa in a nondescript corridor.

After a five-minute wait he was met by a young man in an open necked shirt and off-the-peg suit who introduced himself as Rodney and led him off to his meeting.

Behind the Georgian facade of Whitehall, the interior was modern and open plan. Desks were divided by low partitions, some of which had been personalised with pictures of children and animals, despite his host telling him that everyone hot-desked.

Rodney kept up a dialogue of inconsequential chat while he'd channelled Michael through a second metal detector, then deeper into the building where he also had to surrender his phone, wallet and keys. He was assured that they would be kept safe and returned when he left.

He was handed a badge on a bright orange lanyard with a photo of himself and a barcode, before Rodney took him along another corridor, indistinguishable to Michael from the others they'd trekked down, which terminated at the door to an ordinary looking meeting room.

The backlit panel on the wall showed it had been booked for Cpt. R. Maddox, 14:00 – 16:00.

'Wait here please,' Rodney said, and left him standing awkwardly in the corridor. Michael watched people busy at their desks. A lady was chuckling down a telephone and scribbling notes on an A4 pad for a colleague to read over her shoulder, while another man was reclined in his chair and seemed to be texting.

While he looked over what could have been any office in the country, he became aware of a desk that was so unremarkable that it stood out, with a cluster of cheap ballpoint pens and yellow pencils in a utility plastic holder. Everything about the desk and its meagre contents suggested the man who sat at it.

Michael thought he'd probably been working in Whitehall since the days when they had 3-digit telephone numbers and a typing pool. A small sign etched in white on black and slotted into a wooden holder said Mr. Jones.

Just then the door to the meeting room sprang open and a short, plump man

Michael estimated to be in his late fifties stood in the doorway.

'Ah, Michael is it? So nice to meet you, good of you to join us. In you come, shall I do the introductions now that we're all here?'

Looking around nervously Michael took in the plain office furniture and the people seated around the table. His colleagues for this project.

'Michael do take a pew, I'm Captain Maddox, I'm notionally in charge of this rag-tag committee,' he announced to a smattering of nervous laughter.

'Over here is my second in command for this project, the person who, frankly, does most of the hard work, this is Jane. She's Royal Navy and here because the senior service has our subject in their custody, passed over from the Police last week.'

Jane looked like she'd come straight from a photo shoot for Country Life. Clothes that Michael thought of as rugged, much like her complexion he thought. Her hair was tied back in a perfunctory way with stray hairs falling over her ears.

He couldn't help but notice the relaxed atmosphere in the room, particularly radiating from the Captain. He had been thrown by the utilitarian inside of the building, more like an office on a business park in Slough than the seat of Government.

The Captain continued. 'Now this is Chief Inspector Gunnersby of the Met. He works undercover with some rather unpleasant members of our society, so forget you've seen him eh.' The Chief Inspector smiled dutifully at the joke he'd probably heard 100 times before, and nodded in greeting to Michael.

'Next to our boy in blue, or rather not in blue, is George. He's from the government and doesn't seem to care who knows it.' The Captain smiled at him, George returned the grin and turned to Michael.

'Good to meet you, I'm part of the civil service, seconded to security and working with the joint forces operations committee. It's not so much hush hush as rather dull dull, but anyway that's probably enough from me. Captain...'

'Thank you. Lastly Michael, I'd like you to meet Major Rankin. This is his project really, he will brief us fully, but before he does, everyone has read your file Micheal, but just to recap, you are a clinical psychologist, Bristol university, nothing exceptional but now chugging along nicely in, where was it again...?' He affected to look at his notes and said, 'Harrow, community team, based in... ah Harrow, of course. Knew a few people who went to school there, nice place?'

It took Michael a few seconds to realise this was a question.

'Err, the School or the town?' he asked, 'I've not been to the school, although I've treated a couple of people who work there...the town is okay I suppose.'

'Hmmm, quite' said the Captain, displaying no interest whatsoever in what Michael had said.

'Specialise in children's work, trauma, abuse, loss, that sort of thing?'

'Yes, I suppose so, it's more complicated than that but...'

The Captain cut him off with a smile and wave of his hand.

'Quite so, quite so. Now Jane, your turn I think.'

'Little of consequence. A few internet searches for porn sites but nothing of concern. Bank account steady, no big payments in or out. Rented flat in Willoughby Chase, Harrow. No defaults noted. Breaking even I'd say and lifestyle pretty much what you'd expect.'

Michael was about to protest when the Captain stepped in.

'All in good time Michael, you'll understand this is a matter of some importance and we must be sure we can trust you. Please continue Jane.'

'No complaints at work, member of the UNITE Union but not active aside from paying his subs, pension up to date, no intimate relationships. No close friends, occasional socialising with colleagues. Finances okay.

'Not married – separated from long term girlfriend about 16 months ago, her finances and lifestyle consistent with circumstances. Slight concern over her new boyfriend, has some debt issues but it seems manageable.'

'Michael, anything to add?' Asked the Captain. They'd all seen Michael bristle and when the boyfriend was mentioned.

'How...wait no, why? Why do you know all this and why am I here? I was invited to a meeting about a job by a very persistent chap who just said it would be good for my, and I quote "stalled" career.'

'Ah yes, we probably should get around to telling you the full story.'

***

The hood was removed after a short time and he was unshackled, responding to sharp commands to stand up, stay still, look straight ahead and not to move until he heard the door close. Although his English was good, his earlier questioning was in his mother tongue with the faintest of accents.

His cell was like any other, dull grey walls, metal bed with a thin mattress, a metal toilet and basin with a single towel and bar of soap. Everything was polished, even the inside of the toilet shone.

Military, he thought and mentally he began to reappraise his options. This wasn't going to be a simple charge in front of a bored magistrate, skipping bail and a few months out of the country until things died down.

He was beginning to think he might be in serious trouble.

***

'Michael, we do indeed want you for a job. We'll get to the details in good time. Major Rankin, over to you.'

With no preamble and without referring once to any notes Major Rankin started to speak in a soft voice. Michael assumed he was a man used to being listened to without having to assert his authority.

'You'll be aware from recent news reports that some thirteen girls were recently removed from a property in Hammersmith. They range in age from nine to twenty-one. Mostly underage and working as prostitutes for a criminal gang based in Serbia. Chief Inspector Gunnersby led the task force that resulted in the raid.

'In total we've made twelve arrests, only two directly involved as far as we know, a couple of security guys of no particular interest to us and a few punters caught in the raid.

'Of particular significance is a man we found in a flat above the main premises. At first, we thought he was unconnected with the enterprise, although clearly, he'd have been aware that he was living above a brothel. By chance one of Gunnersby's officers had the foresight to stamp out a fire burning in the grate when they entered his premises. Chief Inspector...'

'Thank you.' The Chief Inspector stood up to talk. A tall and overweight man with what remained of his hair swept over an otherwise bald head, he picked up a manilla file, glanced at the contents then looked straight at Michael.

'We found several items of interest and our forensic team were able to recover documents that indicate the man we have in custody is a high-ranking member of a Serbian crime syndicate who appears to be closely associated with their upper hierarchy.'

Michael wondered why he bothered to stand up and consult the file before such a brief turn. Major Rankin remained seated and continued, again without notes.

'Our sources now suggest that the man in question is not only a decision maker but an accountant of sorts and was using the premises as a safe house while travelling between enterprises. It stands to reason that he is in a unique position to understand the enterprise and how it fits together. In short, he is an enormous asset to us, or could be.'

'Quite so,' said Captain Maddox. 'The Major here has been modest in his assessment. The man in question is, we believe, the key to unlocking a major Serbian crime syndicate, drugs, arms, money laundering and girls,' etcetera, etcetera, and Gunnersby and George here tell me that initial indications are that his position and skill set hiding and laundering money gives him access to other crime networks.

'He is in fact an asset that comes along once in a blue moon, if that. Jane, back to you I think.'

'We have confirmed his name, history, including low level crime as a teenager, gang associations and military career. He appears to be who he says he is.'

'Thank you. Well Michael that's a lot to take in, I'm sure. Apologies for the clandestine nature of the arrangements but you need to be aware that while we have our source in custody plenty of people are searching for him and I'm afraid lives could be at risk.'

'Lives at risk?' said Michael.

'Yes, specifically ours. Of course, we all live with that on a day-to-day basis, but it'll be new to you. You have no more knowledge than you need, no names or anything like that, and we'll keep it that way. I'm sure you have lots of questions but for now let us take a break and refresh our cups then we'll tell you how you fit in.'

Rodney appeared carrying a tray laden with a cafetiere and teapot which he placed on the table. The rest of the meetings participants started chatting, making small talk about department cuts and how good the coffee in Whitehall was.

Rodney was serving but broke off to accompany Michael to the toilet. On the way he kept up a dialogue about the weather.

Standing at the urinal Michael was struck by the mundane poster about maintaining healthy fluid levels while he was grappling with his apparent involvement with the security services and criminal underworld. Little of what he'd heard had really sunk in. Rodney had withdrawn to a discrete distance, although always keeping him in sight, but as soon as he'd washed his hands Rodney resumed his constant, inane dialogue.

Back in the room Captain Maddox greeted him with a cheery, 'Ah, all back now, let us continue.'

'Michael, I know this is bewildering to you and all a bit of a shock. What follows won't be any easier but do please listen and understand the importance of all of this to our security and the good Chief Inspector's efforts to bring down a rather large criminal enterprise.'

Michael started to wonder if he was selected because they thought him expendable.

***

The medical was conducted in English, efficient and unquestionably military. More commands that left no option but to comply. Two escorts in neat grey tracksuits looked ready to force him to cooperate if necessary.

The Doctor asked him about his heart and breathing and left him standing naked while he questioned his medical history in detail. They gave little away, but he formed the opinion that they were homing in on something that concerned them.

He felt he was fit for his age, not overweight and the scars he shrugged off with indifference, simply saying he couldn't remember where most of them came from. The ugly raised scar tissue on his arm he said was an accident at work when he slipped on ice and was impaled on a fence post. It was easier than explaining the knife fight in his teens and subsequent ministrations of a short-sighted back street doctor who'd sold his glasses for vodka.

***

'I'm expendable,' Michael said, 'Just a sap with no ties who you can sacrifice to the Russian mafia if necessary'.

'Beg your pardon?' Said Captain Maddox.

'You want me to work with you because I have no ties, no family waiting for me to return from work, no one to put dinner on the table or to miss me when I'm gone. What is it you expect me to do? Assess this chap to see if he can withstand torture?'

'I assure you; we are capable of assessing people for interrogation Michael.' This was from Jane.

'Quite so.' Captain Maddox said, continuing, 'As Jane points out, we can take care of those arrangements. We want you for something more...subtle.

'To pick up on your previous question, your status as single and...well unencumbered by the complexities of a busy social life, makes you less likely to confide in people. We know you can keep mum professionally Michael and that's important. Oh, and they are Serbian, not Russian. Close but a world of difference. Clear?'

'I guess...'

'Good, so to business. The gentleman we have in custody is currently at a secure site courtesy of the Royal Navy and has indicated that he is willing to make a deal. We are confident that he has enough information to significantly set back organised crime by years. He is, we are in no doubt, an asset to be nurtured and exploited. Jane, would you like to add anything here?'

'Only that interrogation by the Police has gained us very little except a few tidbits thrown their way to encourage a deal. When we received him into our custody it was for the purposes of enhanced interrogation, but we hit a snag.

'After a medical examination it appears our guest has a rather weak heart. A genetic condition he seems unaware of, exacerbated by smoking and drug use, but it does put him at risk if we put too much pressure on.

'You may be asking yourself what all this means Michael and what it has to do with you,' Captain Maddox added to a nod from Michael.

'We need to cut a deal. George has the details worked out but what you need to know is that our 'guest,' as Jane so elegantly put it, has rather specialised tastes when it comes to his, pleasure.

'Given the material we found on his laptop he is in no position to argue. You may think this gives us the upper hand, but of course he holds information that we want, so he thinks he has the advantage. With me so far?'

'Yes, I think so, although I still don't see where I fit in.'

'Quite, but it's vital that you trust our intelligence and that you understand just how important his testimony will be. In short, we need him more than he needs us. He's compromised in the eyes of his employers so if he says nothing he goes to prison for a long time, where they'll catch up with him in time.

'If he is released, well it won't take them long to find out what he's told us and frankly it'll make Jane's team of interrogators seem like a walk in the park, no matter how enhanced they are. George over to you.'

George was lean and tanned. His suit was not off the peg and his whole aura was of calm detachment. Everything about him screamed military except his apparent civil service job. He leant forward and addressed Michael directly.

'We are prepared to do a deal, and to do so we need leverage, something to trade with our man. From our position we can offer him a new identity and as much protection as that can bring him.

'In a hotel suite down the road from here is a young girl we found during the recent raid. Her name is Marsha, and she is about 10 years old, although we cannot be certain, and she doesn't seem to know for sure either. Your task is to meet with her and give us an honest assessment of her mental wellbeing and the benefit of your experience. There will be a translator present and a member of my team....'

Michael stuttered to protest but was

cut off by George raising a hand to cut him off.

'We can dispense with any protocols about third parties being present and suchlike. She is a young vulnerable girl with no English. You will follow our procedures, give us your verbal report back here in three hours, no written reports but you may take notes that will be placed in the custody of your minder and returned to you for the duration of our next meeting. Is that clear?'

'Well, no, frankly that's not anything like enough time, I'll make no meaningful progress and I'm really not sure what you expect me to find out from her.'

George had evidently said all he was going to say on the matter and sat back.

Captain Maddox broke the silence. 'Fair point Michael, but time is not our friend, and we need your report. We've seen your work, you are good at making initial impressions and summing up patients with complex histories and multiple diagnoses. That's all we need.'

He stood up, prompting a scraping of chairs around the table as everyone else did the same, exchanging brief goodbyes as they filed out. Only George stopped on his way out and reminded Michael that he'd see him in three hours' time.

As he stood up Michael wasn't

surprised to find Rodney at the door, armed with a notepad and a selection of cheap ballpoint pens. 'This way' he said, heading back along the corridor and leaving no time for questions. As he leant into a wall to allow a man pushing a trolley loaded with post to go past, Michael noticed that Captain Maddox was following a few steps behind.

'Good morning, Sir,' the man addressed the Captain, who responded in kind then smiled at Michael and gestured to him to continue following Rodney as soon as the trolley had passed.

***

The man raised from his narrow bed. He wore a blue tracksuit that they'd given him after a body search and a shower under the constant gaze of two soldiers and another man who spoke his language fluently.

He was convinced now he was in military custody, the bearing of the men guarding him, their icy politeness and clean-shaven faces marked them out from his business rivals, and the police raid had seemed chaotic enough to be real police. For this, he was thankful. There was an opportunity.

He had explained to the man who spoke his language about his business and his connections. Every so often he would write on a pad of paper, rip it off and give it to one of the guards who would open the door and pass it to a person unseen on the other side.

It was clear the mirror was one way, allowing people to watch and he assumed everything was recorded, although since moving to this new place no mention of being under arrest, reminders it was being recorded, or offers of legal representation had been forthcoming.

He had asked to make a phone call at the police station, and they'd said that it wouldn't be possible and had continued taking his fingerprints. He didn't know who he'd have called if they said yes, but it confirmed to him that they might know his value. It seemed to him that they'd come to a tacit agreement that if he didn't ask, they wouldn't need to refuse him an explanation.

He knew his options were limited, he realised that his very survival depended upon staying in custody until he could disappear. Now the military were holding him he understood that could only happen by mutual agreement.

Fortunately, he had plenty of

information to share. For the right price.

***

Michael returned from his session with Marsha, ushered by Rodney and a young woman in a trouser suit who had been with Marsha when he arrived along with another, older lady and a man in tweed who had translated.

The interview was difficult. The hotel room was furnished for couples on a city break, not bored 10-year-olds. A box of what looked like charity shop toys parked in the bay window appeared untouched.

Rodney had dismissed the older woman, leaving the young woman and translator in the room with Michael and Marsha. The woman, Michael decided to call her the Agent as she was never introduced, had presented him to Marsha and turned to Michael and told him to begin.

Marsha had sat uneasily in a bucket chair for the duration of the session. She looked tired, her eyes heavy and her long hair hung lifelessly down her back. Even when the awkwardness of talking through a translator had worn off, she spoke only to answer questions and never volunteered anything extra.

Michael had seen children like this before, after severe trauma, when they closed in on themselves, becoming insular and cautious of everything beyond their direct control, which essentially meant they lived inside their own mind.

***

The person leading the questioning, the one who spoke his language so well, fiddled about with the back of a TV monitor. He apologised for keeping him waiting as he did so. So polite, the man thought, even when they have the upper hand.

They had discussed what they could trade with each other. Deals were hinted at, information teased out, but both held back from committing too much too soon.

The man admired this technique. He had been present at plenty of negotiations in his lifetime. Some were simple, one party lived or died depending on the result, or thought they'd live even if that promise was subsequently withdrawn. Sometimes it was the choice to die quickly or in agony.

Other negotiations concerned money and 'product' traded between gangs. The product may be human, drugs or money, but it was always traded according to market forces and how important it was for the other party to remain in business.

Deals were done by men who knew the exact value of human life, and that included the value of the people in the room doing the negotiating.

Here in this quiet room in a military prison a man was tinkering with wires to a monitor while apologising for keeping him waiting, a man who never raised his voice, seldom challenged his questions and when he did just asked him if he...

'Wouldn't mind please recapping, I seem to have got myself a bit lost...'and was unfailing courteous to him.

But still he seemed somehow much more sinister than most of the hard men he'd met in his trade.

'Ah, there we are. Now I just press this' he said and pointed a remote controller at the screen.

A room appeared on the screen, showing a single chair in front of a small coffee table.

'What is this for?' He asked his interrogator.

'We're just checking the equipment works to our satisfaction. In a minute or two you'll see them on the main screen.' He turned his head and addressed someone unseen through the mirror.

'All good, thank you all. Please run

VT.'

Turning back to the man he continued. 'Perhaps I can get you a coffee?'

***

'I understand it all went well? Captain Maddox led off as soon as Michael had taken his seat.

'As well as it could go under the circumstances. I'll need much more time if we're to make any progress though. We barely scraped the surface today.'

'I think we all understand the difficulties, Michael. We're not interested in what you couldn't do. Please share what you got from today?

A little affronted but realising his protestations would lead him nowhere, Michael looked at his notes that Rodney had placed in front of him.

'She displays symptoms of trauma, psychological, but physical abuse is likely too because of her known background. Despite the problems of working through a translator I'd say she is close to being catatonic. Her withdrawal from her surroundings, appalling though they were, needs to be managed carefully. She has had people make decisions for her; her childhood was probably spent largely as a surrogate adult. I doubt she knows how to play or socialise.'

Jane raised her hand and leant forward in her chair to address Michael directly.

'So, PTSD?'

'Post Traumatic Stress is a factor certainly, but it's different for children, they haven't got the experience or intellectual maturity to respond to conventional talking therapies. The plus point of course is that they are very adaptable and can, with the right help, adjust.

'They will need constant supervision and usually extra help during their teens. Life's tough enough for teenagers without the extra burden of severe trauma to contend with.'

'Thank you, Michael,' said Captain Maddox.

'Anyone else have questions? Ah, yes Major, you have the floor.'

Major Rankin scanned the papers in front of him with his fountain pen until he stopped at the place he wanted.

'I see here a lot of caveats and, well, one might call them excuses, for not reaching conclusions?'

'I've been given a pitifully short time to prepare, it was rushed, there was no planning for the interview, which was conducted through a translator. The best you can hope for is a preliminary statement outlining where to go next.' Michael said, trying to keep a level tone even though he felt like shouting about the conditions he was expected to work under.

'Quite so,' said Major Rankin. 'But given the circumstances, would you say your conclusions, based on the "pitifully short time..." you had, would apply to others in similar circumstances?'

'The other children in the raid you mean?'

Captain Maddox answered him.

'For the sake of the Major's question, let's assume that we are talking about a group of children aged 9 upwards.'

'Well, they'll all be different. Different backgrounds, differing experiences, and ages, but broadly one can expect traumatic experiences that will present recognisable clinical symptoms, but they will manifest in different ways according to the individual.'

'Thank you Michael,' the Major said, cutting him off. 'So, we just need to wait until we hear from Jane's team.

'Michael, due to the security issues involved, we'd like you to be our guest at a facility nearby. I'm given to understand it is a rather comfortable place.'

'I'm only a few tube stops away, It'll be no problem to go home,' Michael replied.

'We insist. Rodney will take you there, you'll be fed and watered of course, I believe the food is rather good, the salmon comes highly recommended I'm told.'

'Really, I'd rather go home,' Michael said.

'Won't hear of it, you'll be our guest,' the Major told him, as Rodney walked into the room and smiled at Michael.

***

The man looked up from the screen.

'Yes,' he said. 'I think we can do business.'

***

Michael was left in no doubt he was to remain as their guest. No threats had been made, he'd simply been whisked out of the meeting room, straight into a black cab with Rodney beside him and driven to a premises a few streets away.

Rodney took the opportunity to brief him on his accommodation. He told him that meals would be served in his rooms, he'd have toiletries provided and a library and lounge were available. The building was locked for his security, as well as that of the other guests, so he couldn't leave until the morning and no outgoing calls were permitted.

Which reminded Michael. He didn't have his phone back.

'Yes, it's still secure at the offices,' Rodney said, 'we'll fish it out for you in the morning.' and went straight on to tell Michael that breakfast would be at 08:30 and he would be picked up at 09.30 hours prompt.

***

He was told not to worry about anything. No one would take notes because it was all recorded, but he'd be expected to sign transcripts of his statements. The sessions would run daily with regular breaks. The mornings would be used to follow up information he'd given the day before, the afternoons would be reserved for new material. Evenings were free for exercise and relaxation.

He'd remain in custody with three cells accessible to him. One for sleeping, a second for sitting, reading and TV and a third would become available later.

For his security he'd always stay

inside. A rough schedule was approved, and it was agreed that the thanks for his cooperation would be twofold. He would receive a new identity and accommodation at a place to be determined and once his initial information was verified, he'd be allowed access to the third cell.

***

Back at the offices in Whitehall the group had remained in the meeting room while Michael was led away. Captain Maddox stood up.

'Well, everyone happy?' He asked.

The people assembled around the table all gave their assent by nods.

'Excellent. I think we're nearly ready. Major, everything ready your end?

'Yes. The package will be delivered overnight to Portsmouth. Jane will keep us appraised of progress, but we can be fairy sure from initial information that our man is coming up with the goods. Gunnersby's team will be circulating in the bars and clubs keeping ears to the ground, scanning for leaks or other intel, but we're quite confident.'

'So...we seem to be set. George?'

'I've had consent from Downing Street to proceed according to the plan. The

PM is aware of the outline, operational details are the preserve of this room only.'

'Then if there is nothing else, we proceed as planned.' The Captain pressed a button on an intercom on the wall and spoke into it.

'Elisa, red bag please.'

There was a shuffling of papers as a young woman entered the room with a red plastic bag into which all their notes and case files were put.

'Thank you, Elisa, all for incineration please.' Said Captain Maddox. 'Now, I think a meal at my club is in order if you'd do me the favour of joining me as my guests. They happen to supply the food for the safe house where our psychologist friend is spending the night, part of the same building. Word of warning the wine list is a bit limited.

'Oh, and don't touch the salmon, it's dreadful.'

***

'Thank you', said the interrogator, 'you've been very helpful.'

The man thought 'interrogator' was too harsh a word for this man. He was unfailingly polite, even as he described some of the methods his employers used to extract information, or sometimes just to pass the time.

In his own language he would be called *ispitivač*, a much gentler word that suited this man.

'You now have three cells. One has been made into a rudimentary living room, you have your bedroom and here,' he reached into his pocket 'Is a key to the other room.'

'I like your prison' the man said, 'In your prison the prisoner gets a key.' He smiled at the interrogator.

'You have a key to the room set aside for your...hobby. I'm assured that a package will arrive shortly. All three cells are of course secure and guarded.'

'Cameras?'

'In all three rooms and the corridor.' We will be recording you 24 hours of the day, but we won't interfere. Think of it as extra insurance. Will this cause you a problem?'

'Would anything change if it did?

'No.'

'Then all is well. I thank you.'

***

Michael had been annoyed at his incarceration, but he had to admit that the surroundings were convivial. He'd eaten heartily, the room was appointed like a boutique hotel, and if he was honest, he rather liked the feeling of being in a spy film.

He wondered if he'd get more work out of this assignment and realised that this could be the break he'd been looking for. An opportunity to catapult his career up to the rarefied inner sanctum of Government.

Later, as he lay in the double bed and supped on an excellent hot chocolate he got to wondering about Marsha and about the man he'd been told about back at the offices in Whitehall. Something had been niggling at him, a thought he hadn't been able to articulate.

He was feeling sleepy, not surprising after the day he'd had. He took another sip of drink as the worrying voice in his head fought with sleep.

Dimly he wondered if the plan was to give Marsha to the Serbian. The poor rescued girl he'd interviewed, a child brought up to fear and please men, and he, fool that he was, had helped them. He tried to rouse himself but sleep was taking him.

He'd have to raise it with them in the morning.

***

He'd always been good with money. He knew how to make it disappear then reappear in bank accounts as if it had been there all the time, untouched and untraceable.

Before that he had been a foot soldier. As Soviet rule collapsed, he'd been one of the ones to benefit.

The organisation he belonged to had politicians and business leaders in their clutches. On the surface they were charming men in designer suits with expensive briefcases and Italian shoes. Behind them, men like him made sure everyone did as they were told.

He had, he admitted, a penchant for enforcement. He was good at it. He was imaginative and cruel in equal measure. Family members would be kidnapped on his orders to ensure compliance, children taken in exchange for debts, executions were commonplace. The more people were seen to suffer the greater the message. He spread terror and made many people rich, himself included.

He had respect and status, and he had his hobby.

In truth, although his money skills were prized, his reputation was enough to secure good deals and get agreement without argument.

He felt it was a shame he spent so much time wearing a suit and making deals. He missed his days in the country of his birth, getting respect, status.

He missed his hobby.

***

When Michael woke up it took him a while to remember where he was. He stretched in bed and remembered Marsha and what they might be going to do to her. He had to alert someone, maybe he'd go to the police, then he remembered the Chief Inspector at the meeting. He'd go straight to the press. That's what he'd do.

***

The man opened the canvas bag and took out a set of handcuffs, inside he was pleased to see it had everything else he had asked for.

He'd wondered if they would keep their word. He had given them a lot of information, enough to incriminate several key people in the syndicates and the names of some very public figures, including one member of parliament, and he had told them where to look for the evidence they needed.

He still had plenty in reserve, more than enough. Perhaps he'd ask them for another when he had finished with this one.

***

Michael swung his legs out of the bed. He still felt groggy. He'd have to clear his head before he went to the papers.

***

The man picked up the key and felt a warm tingle of anticipation. This is what he lived for. He savoured the moment. Slowly he looked up, rolled his shoulders, winked at the camera in the corner of the room, picked up the bag and walked out the cell door.

***

The tiny room was tiled halfway up and the rest painted magnolia. Light came from a bank of four monitors on the wall.

A small, neat man was seated at the table, in front of him a thin manilla folder, pen and writing pad. He looked up as a figure winked towards the camera, disappeared from one screen, and appeared in another.

He opened a notebook and wrote the date at the top in neat cursive script. For the next four hours he sat impassively in front of the screens, only stirring to make the occasional note.

A routine he was to follow for the next five evenings.

***

The door unlocked and opened leisurely. The man stood in the open doorway, a set of silver handcuffs swinging from one hand. In his other hand he held a canvas bag. He smiled and thought of all the good times he had missed. Now he could indulge with impunity.

'Good morning, Mister Psychologist man. Let me tell you about my hobby,' he said as he took pliers, a hammer, skewers and a set of knives out of the canvas bag.

***

It was only then that Michael understood that it wasn't Marsha they were giving the man...

Cheese and Pickle Sandwiches

2044

The man had arrived on a dirty white horse. Little more than skin and bone it trudged to a faltering halt as the man slid off and dusted himself down. Tethering it to the stump of a tree he pulled down the bags strung over its flank, undid the crude reins made from orange bailing twine and tugged at the blanket that served as a saddle.

Bending down he ruffled its mane, then rummaged in the canvas bag slung over his shoulder, turned, and shot it through the forehead.

2018

The appointment was made by letter, with no return address or other way to respond. That was why two days later the strange man was on Stewart's doorstep.

He was short, almost bald except for a crescent of neatly cut hair and he clearly favoured clothes from the brown end of the spectrum. His tie was fastened with an enormous knot under a collar that was frayed around the neck. Under his jacket he wore an ugly v-neck sweater in defiance of the weather.

His shoes were immaculate, even though he'd walked across the dusty yard to get to the door of the farmhouse.

He even wore driving gloves, Stewart noted with amusement, which he hoped didn't show on his face.

'Good afternoon' the man said, looking down at a piece of paper as he extracted it from a thin manilla file.

'Mr Roberts is it?' he asked, holding out a slightly dog-eared card for Stewart to take.

'Mr Roberts?'

'Sorry, I just had a sense of Déjà vu.' Stewart said, taking the card and giving it a cursory glance before putting it into his back pocket.

'Please, you can call me Stewart.'

'I wonder if we might continue inside, we don't want the neighbours gossiping, do we?'

Stewart followed his gaze as the odd little man looked both ways as if he expected net curtains to be twitching.

'Our nearest neighbours are in Stowmarket, and that's over two miles away,' Stewart said, but he stood aside and gestured for him to enter.

Inside he led the man he now knew from his card to be called Mr. Jones, to the large kitchen table.

'Kettle's on, now, Mr. Jones. Excuse me, I was just finishing my lunch,' Stewart said, as he picked up a plate with the remains of a sandwich on and placed it next to the sink.

'Now how can I help?' he continued, 'I told Tony what I found.'

'Tony being PC Tony Herington?'

'That's him, Tony.'

'Yes, and thank you, that was the correct thing to do, Stewart, but I need to go over it and perhaps ask a few more questions.'

Stewart made them both tea while his visitor was rifling through his briefcase, also brown Stewart noted with a sardonic smile he tried to hide, then settled himself at the table.

'Before we begin,' he said, 'who do you work for again?'

'I'm just a civil servant. I mostly visit local authorities and people in places like this in the lovely Suffolk countryside, compiling reports of, er, incidents. It all goes to an office in London and that's it really. Now, please tell me what you witnessed, in your own time.'

'Well, as I told Tony, I was in the top field checking on the hedges we planted last year...'

'What was the weather like?'

'Hot, don't know what temperature or anything but I know there was no breeze to cool off.'

'I see, and the time of day, do you recall?'

'About noon. I came back for my lunch and that's when I called Tony.'

Mr Jones consulted his papers.

'You called Stowmarket Police at 13.04, where you spoke to PC Herington for 17 minutes and 24 seconds.'

'If you say so. Sounds about right.'

'I'm sorry, I interrupted you. Do continue,' said Mr. Jones, looking up at Stewart.

'I was in the top field, when I found it.'

Stewart thought back to the day in question.

Tony had recorded what he'd told him but despite the young constable looking serious he knew he was sceptical. Why wouldn't he be?

Stewart had once caught a load of students from the agricultural college trying to make a crop circle in one of his fields. Tony had dealt with them by sending a sergeant from Ipswich into the college with a bill for the damage. It was never paid but it had served to stop the outbreak of 'mysterious' crop circles in the area.

At least until now.

'It was a huge circle. I couldn't get up high enough to see properly. My nephew Tommy's got a drone, he's bringing it round on Saturday, after his football practice.

'I see. Did it do any permanent damage to the field?'

'It flattened most of it, but I suppose they're just kids. Are you the man who can sort out compensation? Tony told me there might be some.'

'I'll see what I can do, but events like these, well, there's not really a procedure in place. Now, is there anything else you can tell me?

Stewart pretended to think about it. In truth, there wasn't. It was as simple and mystifying as he'd told the man from the government, or council, he still wasn't clear where he was from. As he recalled, the card he was now sitting on had just his name and a telephone number on it.

'No, that's all really. Seems a lot of fuss really. If it wasn't for the damage to the field, I'd not bother about it.'

***

In Stowmarket PC Tony Herington

was seated in the manager's office of the Co Op. He'd had a visit from a man from the government that morning, a Mr. Jones according to his card. Just a quick courtesy call to check Stewart Roberts address and to thank him for reporting what he'd seen.

Tony wasn't convinced he'd seen anything other than the handywork of some kids. But Stewart was a good friend. One of the most down to earth people he knew so he took his report in good faith and filed it.

Protocol was to pass things like this direct to the RAF, who had a couple of bases locally. Chances were if it wasn't kids, it was something to do with them. He'd done his duty and expected to hear no more of it.

The relief manager beside him was fiddling with the controls of the CCTV monitor looking for the teenagers who she was sure had walked out without paying for their sandwiches and drinks.

'It'll be that lot' she said, pointing at the screen.

'PC Harington? Hello, are you alright?

***

Mr. Jones sat forward in his seat, straightened the papers on the table in front of him and sighed.

'You're a sensible man Stewart. You

didn't make any hysterical calls to the newspaper or invent details. Just facts, and I thank you for them.'

'So, what is it, kids again? Stewart said, stifling a yawn.

'May I just check, have you told anyone other than constable Harington about your sighting?'

'No, and I only told Tony because I thought if it's recorded, I might get compensation when they find out who was responsible.' He yawned.

'Well, that's not so straightforward. Stewart, may I ask, how do you feel, you look a little peaky?'

'Fine. Tired, groggy now you mention it.'

Mr. Jones checked his watch and clicked his tongue.

'You'll be sleepy, your body will begin to feel numb. I'd advise moving to a comfortable chair, Mr Roberts. Easy now' he added as he helped him into a chair by the Aga.

'What's happening to me?' Stewarts words were beginning to slur.

'Don't fret Stewart.'

'The neighbours will have seen you come in...' It was like thinking through fog as Stewart fought to stay conscious.

'Let's not worry about the

neighbours, after all, what was it again?

'Oh yes, the, "nearest neighbours are in Stowmarket, and that's over two miles away." And I don't think your local constable will be in any fit state to assist you now either.

'Things must take time I'm afraid. Your body will shut down slowly, from the outside in, as it were. Vital organs will start to struggle, the brain is the last to go.

'It's called Batrachotoxin. It comes from a species of frog found in South America. Or maybe a toad, now I come to think of it. Anyway, it's from the Amazon. The clever thing about it is that its transmissible by touch and almost impossible to detect.

'Don't worry Stewart, it's very gentle. In the meantime, let me pass the time by telling you a story. I seldom get the opportunity nowadays. Not in my profession.'

***

'My father was a junior diplomat. I never really bothered to find out what he did, he wasn't around much, and my mother was at home anywhere where there was a bottle of wine, preferably two or three. When he was posted to Sierra Leone,

I was packed off to boarding school. His driver left me in the company of a prefect who helped himself to the £5 note the driver had pressed into my hand before depositing me at the bursar's office.

'Of course, I immediately told him about the £5 and he told me to let it go and man up or I'd be eaten alive.

Not the start to my education I'd hoped for, but I quickly learnt. The first lesson being to watch people. I was a quick learner and I soon found out I could survive, indeed thrive, by the one skill I had at my disposal.

'Anonymity. I faded into the background and discovered that a tweak here and a prod there could do wonders for a boy who just wanted to be left alone. That prefect fell down a flight of stairs just before my first Christmas at the school. He mended, after a fashion, but never made the rugger team again.

'The boys who had led the dorm initiation, ritual de-bagging on my second night, found themselves with terrible food poisoning. One might have thought that the tuck shop cakes they took from my trunk had been laced with rat poison.

'In upper school I just disappeared. Some of the Masters didn't even know my name. I wasn't afforded the comradery of a nickname by my peers, nor the use of my Christian name by my house master.

'I was Jones to those who bothered to learn my name, and there were precious few of them. I learnt patience and stealth. How to drift through a room without attracting attention or stand in the shadows and watch without being seen.

'I thought my anonymity had served me well, but there was one master who recognised my talent. He invited me to take tea with him in his study. It was a hot day, must have been around this time of year, and told me he'd been keeping an eye on me, as much as he could, but that I could be very elusive.

'He said I could hide in the open and that, he assured me, was a talent that some people would prize very highly. He hinted at my involvement in one or two 'accidents' but assured me that so long as no more occurred on his watch my secret was safe with him.

'University was...dreary, but my contacts were grateful for any names and information the quiet bloke at the back of the student union could provide. One rather seditious young lady got it into her head to take direct action against her bank, ostensibly because of their involvement in the arms trade, although I suspect she owed them money. Anyway, her plan failed thanks to her home-made bomb exploding prematurely in her flat while she slept.

'My contribution was never acknowledged of course. It's not like the cinema. Just a nod here, a quiet conversation about a troublesome person there and an understanding is reached.'

As he said this, he started pulling his gloves back on, and was interrupted by a gurgle and sigh from Stewart.

'You're a farmer. Big, callused hands, so I think it's wise for me to stay with you, to make sure it works, you can never be too careful. I hope I haven't bored you. One so rarely gets the chance to chat,' he said, removing a glove and gently checking Stewart's neck for signs of a pulse.

'Heart failure in one so young and fit, it's a shame really. I hope Tommy's mother or father come in first on Saturday, I wouldn't want your nephew to be the one to find you.

'Oh, and the circle in your crops, just a side effect of our...experiments.'

***

Mr Jones carefully placed the mug he had been drinking from into a clear plastic bag and put it in his case.

He walked over to Stewart, who was drifting in and out of consciousness and gently tipped him forward and spoke directly into his ear, 'It was on the business card, in case you're wondering. I doubt that they'll suspect it but one can't be too careful.'

He withdrew the card from Stewart's back pocket, laid him back down with care, opened the door of the aga and tossed the card on the dying fire.

Walking to the sink he inspected the remains of the sandwich. 'Cheese and, ah yes, pickle, of course. How dreary.'

Turning back, he said, 'Well, good day Mr. Roberts, until we meet again.'

He touched his forelock and bowed his head slightly towards the body slumped in the armchair, looked around the room one last time, picked up his folder and walked out of the kitchen, closing the front door carefully behind him.

Outside he opened his case and extracted a small notepad and read quietly to himself, tracing each line with his pencil.

'Poison, suicide by shotgun, accident with threshing machine, that was a messy one Mr Roberts, quite ruined my shirt. Let's see, another suicide, fell down the stairs and now...' He licked the end of his pencil, 'Heart attack.'

Everything was still and quiet inside except for the buzzing of a lone fly. The sun shining through the windows lit up the dust dancing on a gentle breeze, the last embers of the fire in the Aga settled. A door creaked as the heat of the day ebbed into the cool of evening.

2019

'Good afternoon' the man said, looking down at a piece of paper as he extracted it from a thin manilla file.

'Mr Roberts is it?' He asked, holding out a card for Stewart to take.

'Mr Roberts?'

Waving the remains of a sandwich Stewart said, 'Excuse me, just finishing my lunch. You can call me Stewart.' He took the card and gave it a cursory glance.

'I wonder if we might continue inside, we don't want the neighbours gossiping, do we?'

'Well, Mrs Barns over the way is no stranger to a twitching net, but I don't think anyone around here is going to worry about me opening the door to a man in a suit. I'll tell them you were trying to sell me insurance.'

'That might be worth considering Mr Roberts, but now, if we might step inside?'

'Of course, sorry, through there, first on the right. I understood from your letter this is about compensation?'

'That is, in a sense correct.'

'That was a year ago, before I sold the farm and moved to town.'

'I let this one play-out a bit further this time Mr. Roberts. The travelling takes its toll on ones body, jet lag with a side order of migraine.'

'So, you do this abroad as well, sorting out compensation?'

'In a way, it's, er...one of my tasks.'

'No wonder it's taken so long.'

Mr Jones sat back in the armchair and pulled a manilla folder out of the briefcase on his lap.

'Mr Roberts...Stewart, may I call you that?' Stewart nodded.

'Good, now Stewart, as I said, it's been a long time. You are too close now to the incident we previously wanted to avoid.'

'Erm, I don't follow you, are you sure you've got the right notes there Mr Jones?'

'Oh yes, quite sure. How is the drinking these days Stewart? You sold the farm because of debts. Making a living out of farming is tough enough, worse when you drink what little profit there is, not forgetting some of your crops being ruined by mysterious circles.'

'Now wait a minute...' Stewart said, leaning forward in his chair, his hands gripped the arms of his chair and his knuckles started to turn white.

'Please Stewart, I am here to help. Not with your drinking, but that has caused us some...issues...which we need to address. Again.'

Stewart was standing up now, and made to step towards Mr Jones, who remained seated and appeared perfectly calm and composed despite Stewart looming over him.

'Stewart, sit down. Nothing you say will alter the facts. I'm here to set things right and...' he was interrupted by Stewart who had opened the door to the hall.

'Leave, now. Forget the bloody compensation, just get out.'

'As you wish,' said Mr Jones standing up, 'But first,' he put the folder back in his briefcase and pulled out a small pistol, which he pointed at Stewart.

'I do hate these, so crude, and hard to cover one's tracks. Now be a gentleman Mr Roberts and take a seat.'

'What the...'

Mr Jones sighed heavily, 'Yes, it's a gun, yes, I'm pointing it at you, yes, it is loaded and yes, I will use it if I must. Let's dispense with the clichés and get back to business shall we…'

***

It wasn't always this complicated, Mr Jones thought to himself as he tied Stewart to the chair with Duct Tape and gagged him with the gimp mask that he had been so embarrassed buying that his stutter had made an unwelcome return.

He did though appreciate the simplicity of it and admonished himself for not buying more, although, on reflection he thought that may have made the thin man with the penis earring ask awkward questions, or worse, attempt some lame joke.

Mr Jones didn't appreciate jokes and when they were made at his expense he particularly disliked them, and made mental notes on ways to dispatch the person telling them.

'Comfortable?' he asked Stewart, who shook his head furiously in response.

'Well, it'll have to do, I don't know why I asked really. Now, although you won't remember, we've met before, several times.

'In fact, I have, er, well, dispatched you a few times Stewart. I have a list if you're interested? No, well, probably for the best. Now, I'm here to see what happens if we delay you rather than deploy more...radical methods.'

He leant back against the wall.

'Time, Stewart, it really is rather odd. You are a drinker and sold the farm because of your mounting debts. You also have a rather lax regard for the law, especially as it pertains to driving while under the influence.

'For example, this evening you are due to drive, while inebriated I hardly need add, to the One Stop convenience store where you purchase a cheese and pickle sandwich, a half bottle of White and Mackay whisky, a Mars bar and on the way out, a bucket of maggots from the vending machine.'

Stewart struggled against his restraints in vain. Settling back, he stared up at Mr Jones, pleading with his eyes.

'Your plan was to spend the evening fishing at Carston Lakes.

'Not unusual for you on a Friday evening, although this Friday, today in fact, your attention wanders and you only see the gentleman crossing the road at the last minute, just in time in fact to witness a not inconsiderable portion of his cranium splash across your windshield.

'No need for the wide eyes and

shaking of the head Stewart, I know it hasn't happened, but it did, or will, or has, or in fact might not.

'I do apologise, our language is a tad cumbersome for explaining time. We were designed for telling stories, wooing and fighting, not necessarily in that order of course, abstract concepts of multi-dimensional time and space were not key to our survival as a species.

'Think of time like a raft on a reservoir that's slowly filling up. The past is below us, the future above and all around us the surface, where water and air meet. That's where we are now.'

Stewart looked as puzzled as a man restrained by a gimp mask and two rolls of duct tape could look.

Mr Jones perched himself on the edge of the sofa and leaned forward.

'One can dive into the past, memories and feelings and what-not. But above is, as yet, unexperienced.

'All you can do is drift along the surface, the water becomes deeper and so you rise slowly upwards, but only enough to experience the threshold between the water and air, never higher up into the air, or, for our purposes Stewart, the future. With me so far?'

Stewart gave no indication of

comprehension, but he nodded with a slight shrug.

'Good, I'm not sure you do understand but pray let us continue anyway.

'Now, imagine a waterspout. Are you familiar with such things Stewart? Good, then imagine travelling up and down that spout, a passage between the present and future, and back again. Such things do exist, my presence here is testament to that.

'Such phenomena, the equivalents of waterspouts, but for time, come about under certain conditions. We've found seven of them. Something to do with dimensions and quantum physics but on a larger scale. I'm sure there are people who could explain this better than I can Stewart.'

Stewart sat impassively. He still had no idea why this strange man was in his house and had wrapped him in tape.

'To continue, a boffin in Siberia cracks the 'spouts' open, in a few months' time. He tampered with quantum physics and after a few days of tinkering...well, it all got rather messy. Nearly made us extinct in fact.

'Once it all settled down, we had ways to port between time. It was all a bit crude at first, finding the spouts and using them.

Finally, after a few rather distressing, let's call them industrial accidents, we harnessed a way to use them.

'Incidentally, they leave a trace not unlike a crop circle, although cruder than all that fancy nonsense students get up to.

'Now, the gentleman whose demise you and a bottle of White and Mackay have been responsible for, so happens to be the one man who is charged with preventing the catastrophe from occurring. Do please pay attention Stewart.

'His name is Macgregor. Clive Macgregor, and aside from living in the Suffolk countryside as a book dealer he happens to be a rather good mercenary and a splendid assassin.

'Now thanks to you, he seems destined to spend eternity being spread over the asphalt of the B134 instead of boarding a Hercules to Berlin and thence onto Siberia by whatever nefarious means he's been arranging for the last 6 months.

'My intervention in the past has ensured he made his flight, several times. Which you may gather is rather confusing because once should have been enough.

'Nothing we could do seemed to alter the fact that, for one reason or another, he failed. If he wasn't struck by you, something would go wrong later. Between you and I Stewart it has all become rather tiresome.

'Evidently fate had other designs on our future so when his last attempt, with grim predictably, failed, we left him there. In the future. I imagine he'll be a bit annoyed, but he is also here about to cross the busy B134. It's quite intriguing don't you think?'

From his position bound to the chair Stewart gave no indication of finding it anything other than gobbledegook, as his mother would say when he had fabricated some obvious lie to explain a broken window or missing portion of cake as a child.

'Which brings us back to tonight. He is both here and in the future.

'Which is all very quantum and impossible. Yet is happening all the same. The timeline is a bit messy but, and here Stewart is your moment to shine, by leaving you alive and preventing you from running him over he shall continue to his no doubt fruitless quest and you shall live free and unburdened by a life at her Majesty's pleasure, with the guilt of a drink driving death on your conscience.'

Stewart shrugged.

'I'm doing you a favour Stewart, as a thank you for all the times I've, well, I've dispatched you.

'Now, I shall return forthwith. In the meantime, do be a good chap and remain where you are. It's for your own good.'

As he was saying this Mr Jones walked around Stewart tugging at the tape. Satisfied, he nodded towards him, collected his satchel, and carefully closed the door behind him.

2045

This close to the compound it was hard to ignore the smell. Standing on the bank of the pass, where the old railway divided the hill in two, the sweet cloying small of death mingled with acrid smoke and sewage. The land was barren, the grass dead and brittle, trees had fallen and crops in the once plentiful fields had been overrun with weeds, which in turn had withered and died.

Within the compound walls, past the barricades of rubble and rusting vehicles topped with sharpened spikes and wire lay what passed for civilisation.

Controlled by a self-appointed Mayor who had risen to the top by leading the most ruthless of the gangs, he gave no quarter and among the victims of disease and starvation piled up around the walls, there lay many who had succumbed to the enforcers within.

His inner sanctum was in the skeletal remains of some vanity office building that was now home to the meting out of rough justice and laws passed by 'Mayoral decree,' posted up at crossroads and on old billboards. Rules for curfew, how much tax to be paid and in what form, how to exchange your stamped work docket for food, and so on. Each decree was effective immediately and ignorance of the latest version was not tolerated.

The rank pile of bodies grew daily. Diseased livestock mingled in with humans who'd been too ill to work or had died from cold, fever or just given up and withered away. Bony arms seemed to grasp from the bottom of the pile. A shawl, ragged and flapping in the wind, hid whatever terror lay swaddled within. Here and there were battered corpses, beaten, and broken by the gangs, whose clubs and sticks were the de facto method of execution.

A slime oozed out, putrid and fowl as it tricked downhill to the dung heaps, piles of human waste tossed over the side by the women who collected the buckets at first light and emptied them on whichever of the heaps was downwind that day. When the women had completed their rounds, they would scrape off as much of the dirt as they could with a blade or flint and then queue for their meal docket.

***

I had been left here. After another failed attempt, what was it five or six now, instead of a hasty retreat and debriefing no one came to my rescue.

I was another victim of the turmoil I was supposed to prevent.

***

A short distance away a couple were seated on a hummock, gnawing at bones, whether human or animal it was impossible to tell.

Lone travellers heading to the compound were seldom let inside unless they brought something to trade. From his vantage point where he had scouted for the last few days, he had witnessed a steady flow of people approach the gate, mostly solo or in small, ragged groups and all had been turned away.

A larger gang would have been driven off by force and evidence of such a battle lay not far from the walls to the east where the bodies lay where they'd fallen. The man had been able to retrieve binoculars along with some water and tools from someone he found dying in a culvert.

As he surveyed the scene below, a plume of smoke spiralled up and was whipped towards him by the breeze. It carried with it the scent of something cooking on an open fire.

He longed for cooked food, but to light a fire would attract unwanted attention. Besides, he thought to himself, he had scant reserves of food and little that would be improved by cooking.

The man was familiar with the compound, having lived there for a few months as life readjusted to its present dog-eat-dog world.

He had bartered his way in with the carcass of a half-starved horse.

As another gang war threatened to engulf the compound, he remained hidden, watching the chaos unfold. From a vantage point high up in a derelict office building, he witnessed the beatings, raping and random acts of violence as the victorious rampaged through the streets.

Neutrality wasn't an option, if your allegiance was suspected your chance of survival was slim to none.

***

By chance a way out of the compound presented itself while I was foraging for food, sticking close to the walls and keeping away from the fires that meant a roadblock or gang members spoiling for a fight.

As I skirted the remains of a derelict department store, I caught sight of a small group being ushered through an opening hidden among debris. I assumed, correctly as it transpired, that this led to the loading bay of the store and thence an exit for scavenging parties.

I clambered through the tunnel in the early morning, chancing that as dawn broke there'd be enough darkness remaining to compensate for the lack of cover beyond the walls, but enough light to navigate by. I had no desire to stumble into one of the pits laid in the clearings beyond the walls. As I stumbled in the flickering light of my stub of candle, I heard voices behind me.

Having been careful to wait for the party to return I guessed this must be a new group. I quickened my pace, and in so doing disturbed one of the pallets shoring up the tunnel as it cut through the rubble of the barricade.

The voices rose to shouts in the echoing tunnel as I picked my way over the rough floor.

The voices grew in volume as I burst panting into the carcass of an old bus, the door of which formed the exit into the barren world outside. Knowing there was no cover beyond, I dived under a seat rank with the pungent stench of animal waste, and focused on controlling my breathing.

From my position I watched as four sets of stout boots milled about by the doorway. Looking closer I could see that what I thought was a pair were mismatched.

Despite my fear, I focused on this anomaly as I lay in wait for my fate. Three men and one woman, judging by the voices, stood discussing what to do with the tunnel and what they'd do to whoever they'd been following.

I could see the studded tips of the clubs they carried. The staff of the group leader tapped impatiently against the seat I was under, confirming my worst fear, that this was a party of enforcers.

They seemed satisfied that no one was beyond the walls and the leader told the rest to search the tunnel for hiding places. I lay still but was sure the beating of my heart would give away my position.

My time was up, precious seconds before I was hauled out, dragged beaten and bloody back through the tunnel or paraded outside as a new sun lifted the darkness from the land.

I prayed for a speedy dispatch, and as I did a low rumble started somewhere in the tunnel behind us, followed by a cloud of dust that tore through the bus and out into the wilderness, followed by my pursuers coughing and spluttering into the grimy dawn.

That part of the tunnel had collapsed was beyond doubt, but I dare not crawl from the safety of my den until everything settled and I was sure that no one was coming back in, which meant waiting until darkness fell with only rodents and insects for company.

I eventually took my chances as the sun went down, before night set and while the cooking fires distracted the lookouts.

***

Outside the man avoided the roads and followed the route of the old railway away from the compound.

While foraging for blackberries he discovered an old railway workers hut amongst a mass of brambles. It was made from preformed concrete slabs crudely bolted together. The door had long since disappeared and the inside was carpeted with guano and the carcass of a dead dog.

With a bit of effort and a lot of cuts he managed to clear it out and weave the brambles into a screen. He walked around the site three times, making minor adjustments before he was confident that no sign of it was visible from the track or fields.

This became home. By alternating his route in and out and always entering the bushes feet first he could cover the entrance after him, to keep the tracks invisible, or at least to look like paths made by animals.

The man could lay on top of the hut unseen, while standing on it gave a good view all around the area towards the compound.

In the other direction he could see up to the tree line that marked what had once been a river that had carried narrow boats and pleasure craft to a once thriving market town, but was now a festering stream, gurgling through mud, sewage and waste of all kinds.

Beyond the remains of the lock had been a basin full of boats, and further downstream where nice houses gave way to warehouses and industrial units was the old port where coal and livestock had been traded.

A rusting hulk that had once been

home to a troop of Scouts was the only vessel now, listing to port in the silt. It had no functioning engine so wasn't used for the evacuation.

A few weeks into the ferocious summer, three months after his escape from the compound, he was permanently hungry. Food outside was practically non-existent.

Foraging parties from the compound took what they could, the sun shrivelled what remained of any fruit and vegetables abandoned in gardens and orchards and even the rabbits and rats were in short supply.

He edged ever closer to the compound, trying to find a weakness, a way to get something to eat without becoming one of the wretched people in their rags picking over the piles of flesh on the perimeter.

***

Eventually, I realised no none was coming to extract me this time, so I made the best of it.

It was my fault after all.

***

Some said it was an act of God. Some a nuclear war or the result of an experiment gone wrong. Others declared it an attack by aliens or mother nature fighting back against us.

It took less than two weeks for the façade of civilisation to crumble. Education, medicine, agriculture and all the other veneers we used to mask our animal instincts disappeared, along with large chunks of our known world.

Yosemite exploded and the sky turned grey. Japan fractured and burnt, along the Pacific Rim cities crumbled and islands were lost while others were born from bubbling lava.

The chaos spread. Long extinct volcanoes started smoking, dormant fault lines rumbled and the ground split and folded. No continent escaped the seismic activity.

As the dust began to settle, tremors and aftershocks multiplied, valleys split open, towns were swallowed, tsunamis swept multitudes before them. The sky turned black.

Communications died, the toys and gadgets that had made the world shrink became obsolete. Those left alive in the choking darkness stopped caring about the world beyond their doorstep.

After the darkness came twilight. As survivors staggered out of their refuges it was to stifling dust that hung in the air if the wind was still, or rasped skin like sandpaper when it wasn't. Noxious fumes from volcanos mixed with the sweet stench of death and decay.

As soon as it started it stopped. Save for a few aftershocks and tremors the earth relaxed and settled as grey dust fell for weeks, mixing with rain to coat the ground in a slurry that stifled any growth. Disease spread and the corpses mounted.

The real chaos began as people sought safety in numbers and the protection a group could provide. In time crude compounds spung up, most benign and eager to trade and redevelop a civilisation, but pressure on resources as more survivors sought refuge started to take a toll.

Roving gangs became increasingly savage, so the compounds began fortifying themselves and hiring protection from rival gangs.

Security came at a price though and soon the compounds fell under the control of those hired to protect them.

***

I moved into a compound for my own protection. Amazing what you can achieve with the carcass of a horse that was little more than skin and bone.

I hadn't been in there long before I realised my mistake. Life outside was tough but living under the erratic rule of the self-appointed Mayor and his enforcers became intolerable. We were slaves in all but name, the elderly and infirm were left to starve.

So, I made my escape for a while, but dwindling natural resources and the threat of a cold winter ahead drove me ever closer back towards the compound.

***

Around the world societies were forming, some prospered, after a fashion, while others died.

Violence had become the new currency. The weak were subjugated, becoming slaves in all but name. What had once been taboo became the norm, cannibalism, murder, rape as a weapon, the brutalisation of children. The survivors became ruthless and cruel.

Nomadic gangs started to settle. Babies were born into a world of grey ash and scarce resources. Disease took thousands, hypothermia took the old and weak.

Authorities, civil and military, tried to regain control. Some fared better than others but even the smallest states could only claim a small portion of their territory as truly under their power. Anarchy was always at the border and insurrection a meal away.

The gangs ruled in the wastelands, the areas the authorities couldn't reach.

***

The man spent the summer in the railway hut, but as the breeze brought the scent of autumn and evenings turned colder, he found his supplies were dwindling.

In desperation he ventured nearer and nearer to the compound, dodging the enforcers and foraging parties, looking for something, an opportunity to snatch a foragers unguarded sack or to get into the compound and chance his luck.

Maybe hunger and dehydration caused him to fall asleep on the knoll. When he awoke a man in an ugly brown suit was standing over him.

'Wakey wakey, it's time to talk.'

***

I should have stopped it. I could have too. I had my chance, but assassination relies on split second timing and an absence of emotion.

The face of the scientist smiling at his tiny daughter as he tied her hair in bunches and his wife padding through the apartment gathering up schoolbooks and clearing away the debris from breakfast perplexed me.

Why blow up an apartment block and take all those innocent lives when I could take him out as he left the building?

***

'Mr Jones, I should have known. It's been a long time.'

'He left through the tunnel that linked the apartment to the laboratory this time.'

'I figured as much. Thank you.'

'You look dreadful, may I offer you some lemon barley squash? I have some...er...' He took a Tupperware box from his satchel and examined the contents, 'cheese and pickle sandwiches. Really, you'd think occasionally they'd be more creative.'

'Are you here to finish me off or to

take me back at last?'

'Well, that's awkward Clive, may I call you Clive? Thank you. We seem to have failed in our mission. To be precise, you failed.

'We have been taking care of your unfortunate accident and thus far, despite our efforts, well...'

He looked around with an expansive gesture, 'It all seems to have been in vain. Every attempt has ended in failure. We are resigned to the fact that they always will.

'He leaves by the tunnel, or the explosives fail to detonate, faulty electrics on the trigger, flights delayed due to weather, on one occasion you tripped over a loose paving slab and missed the rendezvous. Honestly Clive, I am beginning to suspect divine intervention.'

'So, you decided to leave me here?'

'That would appear to be the case.'

'So, what now, apart from a rather dull picnic on the wasteland?'

'Now Clive, plan B.'

'Which is?'

'This Clive, this is plan B.' He made another expansive gesture to take in the compound and everything around it.

'This appears to be our future. Every effort to put it back on track has failed, maybe celestial providence, maybe incompetence, maybe sheer bad luck but here we are. Post apocalypse and eating cheese and pickle sandwiches while we wait for the inevitable. Mayonnaise?'

'The inevitable mayonnaise?'

'Very droll Clive. Would you care for some mayonnaise, it might add a soupçon of moisture to an otherwise rather dry sandwich.'

'No, thank you. You said inevitable?'

Mr. Jones dusted crumbs from his suit and laid his satchel aside. He took a sip from his flask and placed it neatly on the ground beside the Tupperware container and looked over at Clive Macgregor.

'The consequences of the catastrophic experiment you didn't stop are dormant for now, but we've detected seismic disturbances that suggest this relative peace is the eye of the storm.

'There is another season of volcanoes and earthquakes on the horizon and this time I fear the damage will be worse. Terminal in fact.'

'Because I failed?'

'Because, for reasons we've touched upon, you don't seem destined to succeed. I've long ago abandoned the church, but frankly Clive, I'd pray. There seems to be nothing else to do.

'Now, please keep the sandwiches

and squash, but I must insist on retrieving the Tupperware, they get very cross in the canteen if I misplace them.

'Are you sure I can't tempt you to the mayonnaise, they seem to have a boundless supply of these little sachets, so they won't miss them?'

'I'm good for mayo ta. So, I'm not coming back with you?'

'Afraid not, not this time. I'm just checking in to complete the paperwork. We're a tad nervous that the portals will close when things liven up again. Now, I must bid you adieu, there is a gentleman in a rather dingy flat trussed up with a glimp mask...'

'I think you mean gimp mask.'

'Ah yes, probably. Anyway, he'll be a bit miffed if I don't release him soon. I must rush, the portals have been closing. There's only two left now and number six is a bit wobbly.'

With that Mr Jones stood up, pulled his cuffs down and brushed crumbs from his trousers.

***

I didn't see him go. He wandered away along the old track and by the time I was up and chasing after him he had vanished.

Later that evening I heard what I thought was thunder, but it rumbled on and as darkness fell, I could see the glow from distant eruptions.

***

2019

Mr Jones waited in the hallway for 15 minutes.

Satisfied that no one was moving about, he crept into the living room and was gratified to see Stewart still taped to the chair.

'Mr Roberts, Stewart. Thank you for waiting for...' he looked at his watch,' One hour and 43 minutes, or in my case, 26 years one hour and 43 minutes. I do apologise for the inconvenience.

'Now I shall release you forthwith, but I urge you to show restraint. Normally I would terminate our relationship at this point but on this occasion, as you haven't done anything wrong, my employers would make a terrible fuss if I did.

'Mr Macgregor will have made his rendezvous unscathed by your attention. It appears he will be in vain and in a few days...well, you'll find out soon enough.

'Please don't go thinking that you'll tell anyone about our encounter. After all Stewart, who will believe you?

'Do we have an agreement, Stewart? A nod will be adequate confirmation.'

Straining against the tape Stewart bent his head forward.

'Capital. I shall cut your bonds forthwith.'

Mr Jones busied himself packing away the evidence of his presence, and Stewart's incarceration, humming to himself as he went along.

Stewart shook his hands and flapped his arms to get his circulation going, then turned his attention to his legs, massaging them each in turn.

Standing up, he fell forward and stumbled towards the wall. Leaning back against it he cleared his throat to get Mr Jones attention.

'He had to invent it, in order for your fellow, Clive was it? Mr Jones nodded. '...to have the technology to stop him. Because he failed the first time, nothing else could possibly work. It's a parathingy.'

'A paradox. I do believe that you are correct. Hmm, there is more to you than I perhaps gave credit for Mr Roberts. Sadly, the only conclusion then is that between you and Clive you have doomed humankind.

'Now, before I go, may I tempt you with some of these pouches of mayonnaise? I find them most convenient for picnics. An ideal tonic for a lifeless cheese and pickle sandwich.'

2045

Clive Macgregor sat on the lonely hill and surveyed the compound and the wastelands surrounding it.

This had been his home for some years now, since the day the earth erupted.

He had no family that would miss him, an ex-wife, and a sister he seldom saw living in the Wirral with a bloke she met at high school. He had no idea if they'd survived or not and had to admit to himself that he really didn't care.

Mr Jones had been an irregular visitor to his shop in Suffolk before the catastrophe occurred. He gave him occasional assignments, and until the last one he'd been thorough and professional.

Clive could feel the occasional shockwave now, the distant eruptions were faint, but dust and ash was swirling about, the sun weak and hazy.

He watched the commotion in the compound and sensed tension in the air.

With a resigned shrug he picked up a cheese and pickle sandwich and took a bite.

'Not bad,' he said to himself. 'Could be improved with some mayonnaise though.'

He scrabbled around on the ground and found a sachet which he bit open.

'Thank you, Mr Jones,' he said, raising half a cheese and pickle sandwich with mayonnaise in mock salute.'

**

Twilight moved swiftly to darkness.

There would be no morning.

The Weight of Sin

Ray Canham

The Weight of Sin

The eerie calmness of that simple chapel made her nervous. There were no windows and just a simple crucifix hanging on the wall.

When invited to take her place at the lectern, she tried to show more confidence than she felt. She looked straight down the camera lens, forced a smile, took a deep breath, exhaled slowly and spoke.

'The reading is from Hebrews 12, verses 1-29.'

***

In the general election of 2030, the sitting Conservative party was punished by voters for successive scandals over the conduct, both personal and professional, of several ministers.

The Labour party failed to capitalise due to infighting over the direction of the party and the Liberal Democrats gained some ground but chiefly served to split the Conservative and Labour votes even further.

Nationalists gained significantly in

Scotland and Wales while Northern Ireland returned to power sharing with an almost 50/50 split.

In England the Nationalist Alliance, fighting its first election and backed by seemingly limitless money from a right-wing evangelical church in the USA took power in coalition with unionists from Northern Ireland and several right-wing members of the Conservative party, who switched allegiance to help them secure a majority.

The King's speech to Parliament promised a crackdown on law and order, and the formation of state Nationalist Alliance youth brigades in all parts of the UK, with an emphasis on 'muscular Christianity.'

They went on to promise an overhaul of the curriculum in state education, from pre-school to colleges, the dismantling of 'socialist' principles governing the national health service and the introduction of mandatory health insurance, the repeal of gay marriage and equal opportunities legislation, a feasibility study into national service and an immediate cessation of abortions except in cases of clear and uncontested threat to the life of the mother or evidence of disability in the foetus.

The Crime and Disorder Bill was

debated the day after the King's speech using emergency powers to combat 'insurrection and rebellion' following widespread protests after their election.

Included in the bill was the immediate restoration of the death penalty for a list of crimes that included murder, treason and injury to a uniformed representative of his Majesty's armed or civil services and members of Parliament.

Provision for hanging was made at three prisons in England while in a fourth, the newly opened and privately run Gateshead super prison, construction started on a special 'death row', using a design and punishment approved by the Minister for Justice, formally a leading member of the British National Party.

Her approval for the prison and its operation gave the company running it, an off-shoot of the evangelical church who had bank rolled her party's election, the right to install its own techniques for managing incarceration and execution.

***

'Therefore, since we are surrounded by such a huge crowd of witnesses to the life of faith, let us strip off every weight that slows us down, especially the sin that so easily trips us

up. And let us run with endurance the race God has set before us. We do this by keeping our eyes on Jesus, the champion who initiates and perfects our faith. Because of the joy awaiting him, he endured the cross, disregarding its shame.'

George Anderson was a lay preacher, an active member of his church and the governor of Gateshead Prison. His father had been a Baptist preacher and had ruled the family home with a firm hand. He hadn't spared the rod, but unlike his older brother and sister, George took a comfort in the strict household and far from rebelling like they had, he embraced a life of hard work and service to the Lord.

He had lost his wife Alice to breast cancer when she was 32, a year and a day after her diagnosis. At the time he was deputy governor of a young offender institution.

He comforted himself that Alice was with her saviour, but he still missed her and felt lonely when he wasn't at work or church. When their only son Luke had gone to university in Edinburgh, he spent all the free time he had at church.

While at Edinburgh studying medicine, the results of the second Scottish independence referendum were announced.

The shockwaves reverberated around the capital and Edinburgh erupted.

Luke was drinking with friends in a pub garden when a wall collapsed as pro and anti-independence demonstrators clashed. He was crushed to death.

The coroner concluded that the demonstrators had probably contributed to his death by fighting across the remains of the wall before anyone noticed Luke.

George took refuge in the church, where he began to find the sermons increasingly banal and 'wishy washy', a term he used with increasing regularity to describe anything he thought liberal in the church.

Weary of the traditional Church of England he joined the Church of the Kingdom of Our Saviour and found a spiritual, and political, home in a newly planted 'super church'.

He immediately felt at home with the no nonsense fire and brimstone style of the American minister, and he particularly liked the emphasis on sin and becoming part of the Lord's army to prepare for the end of days.

Since childhood he'd never doubted his faith. Even when Alice was taken to her reward, he remained steadfast in his belief. If he had doubts when Luke was taken, he buried them along with him.

Thanks to an introduction by one of the congregation he also became an enthusiastic member of the newly formed Nationalist Alliance, donating his time and money to them.

One year after being made governor of a category C prison tucked away in the Suffolk countryside, he told the annual conference of prison officers that it was little more than a holding place for recidivists and white-collar criminals, all of whom took up space, and money, in prison.

He advocated for a short sharp shock prison experience and long-term hard labour for repeat offenders, plus execution for anyone committing murder.

A year after the National Alliance were elected, he was appointed Governor of Gateshead Prison. It would, he was promised, be a model institution, implementing a harsh regime with a Christian ethos throughout.

Central to his plans was a wing prepared for the return of capital punishment. The panel had agreed with George that it was not only a deterrent but a just way of serving the Lord.

When asked about the chance of an innocent person being executed George had replied, 'The Lord doesn't make mistakes...if he calls someone then it is their time. Who are we to question him?'

He started the week before the first prisoners arrived. Some of the guards were old hands but most were recruited from the ranks of the Nationalist Alliance's 'Street Army', as they were known. Young men with severe haircuts who could handle themselves in a scrap and would be ideal for enforcing the code of the prison.

George introduced daily prayer meetings before every shift and sacked two guards during his first week, for insubordination and blasphemy.

As soon as the bill to reintroduce capital punishment passed its first reading in parliament, George started to prepare.

His plans were debated, and he was questioned by the parliamentary working party overseeing prisons and in particular the construction of D wing. Objections were raised but with his church, and not coincidentally it's money, behind him and, as George saw it, right on his side, he won the day.

It would be just, George told the working party, if one allowed for the inmates to dwell on their sins and, he added, allow them time for repentance and to come to the Lord and live with him always. 'I am reminded of Ezekial, verses 9 and 10' he said, 'I will not show pity or spare them. I will bring their conduct down on their own heads.'

He selected prison guards who obeyed without question and whose service to God was, if not exactly cerebral, at least genuine.

They, and they alone would staff D wing, or as he privately called it Luke's Wing. Construction was swift once the technicalities had been sorted out and one year after the reintroduction of capital punishment D Wing received its first four inmates.

***

'Now he is seated in the place of honour beside God's throne. Think of all the hostility he endured from sinful people; then you won't become weary and give up. After all, you have not yet given your lives in your struggle against sin.'

Thomas was brought up in the Jesmond area of Newcastle. His parents were comfortably off and his school years, like his parents and their office jobs, were steady and unremarkable.

He wavered between an apprenticeship in engineering or sixth form college, finally deciding on college because it was on the same campus as the school he was about to leave, armed with a clutch of middling exam passes and a crush on a boy one year his senior already at the college.

With a gang of his school friends Thomas had been among Newcastle United's more vociferous supporters. Chanting turned to scuffles on the street and then to meet ups in quiet pubs with figures who used the terraces as a recruiting ground for young men not afraid of a fight.

By the time he was 17 Thomas was earning a little extra cash providing security for Nationalist Alliance marches and meetings.

He'd never considered church or religion until his nan died. Her funeral was the third time in his life he'd been to church. One carol service at the end of infant school and his cousin's wedding were the other two.

Something said by the minister nagged at him over the next few weeks. So much so that he eventually had it tattooed on his forearm.

'Whatever is not from faith is sin.'

Thomas knew he had sinned. His attractions were a secret known only to himself and God. He joined in the banter with his mates and had a few experiences with women, but thoughts he couldn't quite control welled up unbidden and unwelcome.

Until he looked down at his arm.

His parents had always been liberal in their views and Thomas found himself despising their lack of defined principles. He hated their easy-going nature and found himself increasingly angry at them. The Alliance gave him structure, meaning and a moral compass.

He tried his local church, but the vicar was a woman, and her sermon was all about helping people and being 'nice'. Thomas was fed up with nice. It was too late for nice in his opinion.

By chance he passed the huge hall of the Church of the Kingdom of Our Saviour on his way home. Inside it was bright and airy, the congregation mostly young and welcoming.

He agreed to join a small group of newcomers to the church, which was where he met George. Four weeks later, after the meeting had dissolved into horrid coffee and home baked cakes George offered him a job.

***

'And have you forgotten the

encouraging words God spoke to you as his children? He said, "My child, don't make light of the Lord's discipline, and don't give up when he corrects you. For the Lord disciplines those he loves, and he punishes each one he accepts as his child."

She had expected chaos, noise, cat calling, anything really except the hushed atmosphere inside. The calming green walls, potted plants and carpets seemed out of place in this house of punishment.

Soothing music played in the background, the guards were smart, efficient, and icily polite in the way she associated with the military.

As the first journalist to visit the notorious D wing of Gateshead Prison, Brenda had felt a wave of excitement and nervous anticipation as she approached the gate.

It was a familiar feeling that she came to associate with a big story or when an investigation she had worked on for months finally went to print.

First though she had to pass the protest camp outside the gates. It had been the regular backdrop to news reports from around the world.

One day it was vigils by candlelight, the next might bring communal prayers, protesters with placards and bullhorns or fighting between the campers and pro death penalty marches.

A stone had bounced off her car bonnet and angry faces were pressed against the barriers shouting insults, spit flew in her direction.

A policeman waved her inside, urging her on until the big gates swung open for her then closed just as quickly, sealing her in a security area where she lowered her window and presented her credentials to a young guard.

A security check and pat-down search followed, and she was instructed to deposit her phone and other belongings in a locker. She was handed a pencil and pad then led inside by the guard, who apologised for the rumpus outside and offered to get her car cleaned, adding, 'but you'll probably get the same treatment when you leave.'

Brenda had plugged away, sending polite emails to the Governor that were met with equally polite refusals until, in a last ditch bid she sent a handwritten thank you for his patience with her requests, and thanked him too for standing steadfast in the face of the 'assaults' upon his character in the liberal press.

On a whim she added 'Thank you for doing God's work, may you find peace and courage in your task.'

She wasn't much of a believer. She had attended church sporadically during her childhood and then for a short while as a young student when dating a member of the university Christian Union.

After starting with a local paper filing copy about lost dogs and objections to housing developments, a small inheritance had given her the opportunity to risk going freelance. She soon established a reputation for in-depth investigations into crime and corruption. She was also a lifelong opponent of the death penalty.

She was though savvy enough to know that only the favoured few got access to National Alliance figures and she had worked hard to establish her credentials with them, hiding her true feelings, and her real name, to win their trust.

When activities inside Gateshead were made public knowledge, she abandoned the investigation into the Alliance's finances she had been working on. Instead, she used her contacts to start investigating the mysterious world of D Wing.

A few days after she'd sent her letter, an embossed envelope had landed on her doormat with an invitation from the Governor to be his guest at a Sunday service on D Wing.

Several pages of closely spaced forms arrived the following day; security checks, permission to investigate her background, wavers, and insurances, all to be returned before the provisional offer was made definite and a date agreed upon.

***

'As you endure this divine discipline, remember that God is treating you as his own children. Who ever heard of a child who is never disciplined by its father? If God doesn't discipline you as he does all of his children, it means that you are illegitimate and are not really his children at all. Since we respected our earthly fathers who disciplined us, shouldn't we submit even more to the discipline of the Father of our spirits, and live forever?'

'The human body can normally withstand 50 psi, that's pounds per square inch from a sudden impact.'

'And if that isn't from a sudden impact?' George asked.

'Around 400 psi if the weight is gradually increased. We don't have reliable records, but that's the figure we estimate would be achieved under 'Peine forte et dure.'

'Peine forte et dure?'

'French for "forceful and hard punishment." A board was placed on the accused and weights added. It was commonly used when a defendant refused to enter a plea.

'People would sometimes survive for a day or more. They were even allowed a few morsels of bread and water if they lived for more than that, although the only real mercy ever shown was when people sat on the board to add weight and end it quickly.

'So, this would crush them?'

'Not really, because the weight was gradual, they'd suffocate. Painfully too, with broken ribs and other internal injuries.'

George took a moment to consider this information. The contacts he'd made through his church had finally delivered a response from a matter-of-fact engineer in America into his inbox one rainy Wednesday evening. They were now corresponding regularly.

He sat forward and, after pausing for a moment, started to type again.

'I think we're on to something. Thank you for your time, I'll be in touch.

'Yours in Christ,

'George.'

***

'For our earthly fathers disciplined us for a few years, doing the best they knew how. But God's discipline is always good for us, so that we might share in his holiness. No discipline is enjoyable while it is happening—it's painful! But afterward there will be a peaceful harvest of right living for those who are trained in this way.'

She found herself being led along a bland corridor, one that wouldn't look out of place in a smart office building.

Her escort opened a non-descript door and led her into a tiny chapel. Four rows of six seats were set out facing a small altar, bare except for a simple wooden crucifix. The lectern facing the seats was the only other furniture.

Beside the door she had been led through a camera was being made ready by a guard. He introduced himself as Thomas and dismissed her escort.

'Do the inmates come here for the service?' Brenda asked.

'For their first service only, then they are confined to their rooms. The Governor will be addressing some new arrivals today.'

The door opened behind her.

'Here he is now, Governor – may I present Mrs Brenda Simpson, your guest for today.' Thomas said as George closed the door behind him.

'Thank you, Thomas. Mrs Simpson, a pleasure. Welcome to Gateshead and to D Wing. I hope they've been looking after you?'

George wore a neat grey suit and tie, and he looked good for what she knew to be 62 years old. His hair was thinning but cut well, he wore braces over a crisp striped shirt, and his shoes had the sort of lustre you only got with polish, brushes and lots of elbow grease. His manner too was graceful and affable, Brenda stopped herself mentally using the word charming.

'They have indeed, thank you.'

Before she had time to continue George clapped his hands together and said, 'Excellent, now, I must prepare so may I leave you with Thomas for a few minutes? Our congregation will be with us shortly and I need to check over a few details.'

George made to leave then turned back and said, 'Oh, a thought does occur to me though Mrs Simpson, maybe I can ask you, as a fellow traveller on the road to glory, to honour us with a reading? I have one prepared, if you'd be so good?'

Brenda didn't allow herself time to

think. Years of investigating politicians and big business had honed her ability to respond to seemingly innocent queries that could be traps to catch out the unwary.

'Of course, I'd be delighted.'

***

'So take a new grip with your tired hands and strengthen your weak knees. Mark out a straight path for your feet so that those who are weak and lame will not fall but become strong.'

'A full vending machine, weighing around 1,100 pounds will usually prove fatal, so the plans you sent are well inside margins of error George.

'I wish you luck and God's grace with your project.'

***

'Work at living in peace with everyone, and work at living a holy life, for those who are not holy will not see the Lord. Look after each other so that none of you fails to receive the grace of God. Watch out that no poisonous root of bitterness grows up to trouble you, corrupting many. Make sure that no one is immoral or godless like Esau, who traded his

birthright as the firstborn son for a single meal. You know that afterward, when he wanted his father's blessing, he was rejected. It was too late for repentance, even though he begged with bitter tears.'

***

Thomas gestured for Brenda to lead the way to the lectern. While she fumbled with the sticky note marking the reading, he dragged a chair out of a cupboard and placed it to one side of the front row.

'Mrs Simpson, if you please, when we invite our guests in, I'll ask you to sit here and remain seated while they take their places. The front row will be our new inmates, behind them guards.

'As we are a house of detention, we must observe certain precautions, for everyone's safety. Please don't attempt to talk to or otherwise engage with the congregation in the chapel. If anyone other than a member of staff addresses you direct, please refrain from acknowledging them. We will deal with them.

'Try and avoid eye contact too. I find addressing the camera direct is best when you are reading, otherwise it's a straightforward service. At the end, please remain seated until our guests have left.'

'May I ask a question Thomas?'

'Yes ma'am, although I may not be permitted to give you an answer.'

'Why do you call them guests? It seems inappropriate under the circumstances.'

'I understand ma'am. We are serving the Lord, and we are serving society. The inmates here have time and little else. We're here to make their final days gracious and peaceful, or as much as we can under the circumstances.

'Our mission is to encourage their faith and guide them to the Lord. The Governor is clear that we can achieve more by grace than fear.'

'But isn't their time here spent...' Before she could continue a bell sounded and Thomas asked her to take a seat.

***

'You have not come to a physical mountain, to a place of flaming fire, darkness, gloom, and whirlwind, as the Israelites did at Mount Sinai. For they heard an awesome trumpet blast and a voice so terrible that they begged God to stop speaking. They staggered back under God's command: "If even an animal touches the mountain, it must be stoned to death." Moses himself was so

frightened at the sight that he said, "I am terrified and trembling."

When they had filed in and taken their seats George strode out, a white stole adorned with a simple wooden crucifix over his suit.

Everyone stood up, Brenda taking her cue from Thomas and the other guards, one for each prisoner. One prodded their charge to make him stand.

George smiled and nodded to each member of his makeshift congregation.

'Welcome, to our new guests and to everyone in their rooms. I hope this sabbath finds you closer to the Lord than last week. Welcome too to Brenda, our special guest today and to all our flock of dedicated staff and their families enjoying a well-earned day of rest at home. Please, be seated.

'We have four new guests with us...'

'We're not guests, we're f'ing prisoners sent here to die.'

The commotion was started by a wiry inmate who struggled with his guard until Thomas stepped in. Between them they got him to the floor and handcuffed in one fluid, well-practised move. He was hauled up, still protesting.

Brenda noted that aside from placing a gentle hand on the shoulders of their inmate, the other guards didn't move. Despite her misgivings she was impressed by the quiet discipline on display.

George spoke. 'Mr Higgs, isn't it?'

'What of it...'

'Mr Higgs, you have a choice. You may be escorted to your cell, where you will remain. Or you can stay with us by obeying the rules. I'm sure Tony explained them to you?'

His guard nodded.

'Fuc...'

The blow from Thomas' truncheon to his abdomen was swift. As he doubled up Thomas and Tony hooked an arm under each of his and dragged him out.

'And then there were three,' George said. 'Now, shall we continue...

'Welcome to the chapel. As we worship today, please let us keep Mr Higgs in our prayers, and everyone else who finds themselves here through their sins. Let us be prayerful and ask for forgiveness and wisdom as we join together in this house of correction to praise the Lord. Let us bow our heads and pray.'

***

'No, you have come to Mount Zion, to the city of the living God, the heavenly

Jerusalem, and to countless thousands of angels in a joyful gathering. You have come to the assembly of God's firstborn children, whose names are written in heaven. You have come to God himself, who is the judge over all things. You have come to the spirits of the righteous ones in heaven who have now been made perfect. You have come to Jesus, the one who mediates the new covenant between God and people, and to the sprinkled blood, which speaks of forgiveness instead of crying out for vengeance like the blood of Abel.'

Although they'd kept it as quiet as possible by using contractors linked to the church, and having the labourers sign confidentiality agreements in return for a hefty bonus, rumours seeped out about the unusual facilities in D wing.

Suspicion reached Brenda via a delivery driver whose son was a warden in one of the other wings. She'd started asking around and was met by silence, obstruction or icily polite statements dismissing anything untoward.

When the announcement came, she was ahead of her colleagues in the press, but no less shocked by the gravity of what was proposed.

No, not proposed, she corrected her thoughts as she planned her visit, this was policy, forced through on the back of emergency powers.

HMP Gateshead's brand-new D wing was ready and waiting.

***

'Be careful that you do not refuse to listen to the One who is speaking. For if the people of Israel did not escape when they refused to listen to Moses, the earthly messenger, we will certainly not escape if we reject the One who speaks to us from heaven!'

'After the service, we bring them to their cell.' George was calm and spoke with what Brenda was coming to realise was pride. This was his baby, his crowning glory.

'Court appearances are by video. Occasionally we permit a medical examination but otherwise they are alone. Alone with the weight of their sins.'

'About that, I'm still unclear about the...the way...how it works.'

'Execution. Judgment. Mrs Simpson. Call it what it is.

'These people are felons for whom mercy, except that of the Lord Himself, has been unforthcoming. Appeals have been exhausted.

'They will die Mrs Simpson, as will we all of course. Tomorrow I could be run over by a bus or drop dead from a heart attack.

'Unlike in the examples I've given though, here we give our guests the opportunity to repent. To understand their transgressions and to come to face the Lord and throw themselves on his mercy.'

Brenda glanced at the notebook perched on her lap. It was empty except for a couple of names she'd scribbled in, Thomas and George. She felt a shiver pass through her as she realised she hadn't moved throughout her interview with George.

The man looked like a middle manager. The sort of person who'd put on a tie and cardigan to go to the pub.

'In the court reports they get a year and a day. So, I take it they are...executed after that?' Brenda asked.

'Well, they've been on the path to their own destruction for some time, but yes, I suppose that's how it works. Look, let me show you a cell. Then it will be easier to understand.'

***

'When God spoke from Mount Sinai his

voice shook the earth, but now he makes another promise: "Once again I will shake not only the earth but the heavens also." This means that all of creation will be shaken and removed, so that only unshakable things will remain.'

Antoney Fredricks had been an active member of the Scottish National Alliance since school, and a strict Presbyterian upbringing had mutated into following the Alliance's protestant 'muscular' Christian ways when he moved south.

He had swiftly worked his way up from a guard in A wing to D wing. His first 6 months on D wing were mostly uneventful, even, he admitted to himself, boring.

Today though Thomas, his supervisor and mentor, had invited him to help clean one of the cells.

'Here we are,' said Thomas, as he punched a code into a screen beside the door. Cell 6, The Hay Cell. Day 366.'

***

Thomas and Fredricks pulled on wellington boots over disposable one-piece boiler suits. They picked up a large plastic bag between them and carefully negotiated the stairs to the ground floor of D wing.

They returned twenty minutes later to carry two sturdy oak props, which they carefully laid down outside the cell while they put masks over their mouth and nose and pulled gloves on.

'Ready?' Thomas knew it was Fredricks first one. He remembered how he'd reacted to his first.

'Aye,' the tall Scotsman answered, muted through his mask. He sounded assured but Thomas could see his eyes and they told a different story.

'Then let's go. Remember whatever you see, props up first. They're just a precaution but I for one feel better with them. Then we fetch the bag. There are shovels, scrapers and disinfectant in the bag.

Thomas punched the code into the door and stood back as it swung open. Picking up the first of the props they walked through the open doorway.

***

'Since we are receiving a Kingdom that is unshakable, let us be thankful and please God by worshiping him with holy fear and awe.'

'Ah, here we are. The Coggles Cell.'

George indicated the brass plate on the door, sweeping his hand down to a panel on the wall. At his touch the door swung outwards.

'Who was Coggles?' Brenda asked. 'A wealthy donor?'

'Oh no, nothing so...uncouth. My indulgence if you like. Each cell is named after a variety or music hall star. A time long before us, of innocence and childlike simple pleasures.

Next door we have Hay, after Will Hay, Askey, for little Arthur Askey, and so on. This one is for Burton Coggles, the Chipper Chappie. A pity they don't bring back variety, good clean fun.

'Maybe we'd have more vacancies if our young men and women were exposed to them rather than the vulgar trash of today.

'Please Mrs Simpson, this way' he said, indicating the open door.

'The floor, as you can see, has hygiene facilities built in. A pit latrine it's called. Lighting is from toughened panels in the wall. The one on the right houses a TV screen. A mattress, pillow and blanket are provided. Clothes, food and legal papers are passed through the hatch down here at ground level.'

'So, they are confined here for the duration of their sentence? Brenda asked.

'Yes, to reflect and make their peace. Being alone facing one's fate should focus the mind.

'Remember, some of our guests have been hardened by a life of debauchery and sin. It plates them like armour, and to break that, to let the Lord in through the cracks as it were, well, we need to concentrate their attention on their mortality. On their path to glory.'

'And how do you achieve that? I imagine some of the people here are tough to crack.'

'It's quite straight forward really. The ceiling is stone. 2½ tonnes held by counterweights. Every day of their sentence it lowers by a fraction.'

'Until?' Brenda asked, although with a growing sense of horror she feared she already knew the answer.

'Until day 366 of their sentence Mrs Simpson. Until the weight of their sins has crushed them of course.'

***

'For our God is a devouring fire.'

Fredricks vomited into the potted plant while Thomas finished hosing down the cell.

Thomas felt he owed it to the new recruits to accompany them on their first 'cleaning' operation and Fedrick's reaction wasn't that different to his own first time.

Carefully, they picked up the bag between them and silently carried the remains of the prisoner along the carpeted corridor, with its calming green walls, potted plants and carpets.

***

'Here ends the reading.

'Amen'

Ray Canham

The Wilderness

She said, 'They didn't have any Jacobs Crackers in Sainsbury's. We had to go to, where was it now?'

He said, 'Lidl. Just around the corner from Sainsbury's.'

She said, 'It's very odd, don't you think Lucy?'

Lucy wondered if the oddness applied to the absence of Jacobs crackers or the proximity of Lidl to Sainsbury's, neither of which she felt was newsworthy enough to warrant an opinion.

Eventually they moved on to fuss about the family they had spotted being shown around number 16 less than a fortnight after Mrs Robinson's funeral.

She said, 'It hardly seems right, so soon, her Sharon only wanted the house sold so she can move to Spain. It's no secret.'

He said, 'Well, it never was a secret, she told us at the funeral.'

She said, 'Why Spain though?'

He said, 'Maybe they can be assured of Jacobs Crackers in Spain.'

She said, 'Pass us your plates and I'll fetch the pudding. It'll spoil if we dither in here. Spain indeed.'

Lucy's mother prepared a recipe exactly as directed on the packet. If it suggested 75 grams of rice per person, 75 grams per person went into the pot. She had been known to add or subtract grains one at a time until the scales hit the correct number.

If the instructions stipulated 30 minutes at 180C, then it got 30 minutes at 180C, the oven having been pre heated to the requisite temperature as per directions.

Meals were never an adventure, the weekly menu decided long ago and seldom deviated from.

Of all the ingredients of their established menu, jacket potatoes were the enemy of the fastidious recipe follower. Their insistence not to grow to a standard shape and size meant Mondays quiche might be accompanied by crispy skinned balls of mush or fork bending solid tubers. So long as they had the requisite 1 hour 31 minutes at 190C they were considered ready to serve.

Over the years Lucy had grown accustomed to her Friday evening salmon, boiled potatoes with a knob of butter (20 grams) ½ teaspoon of dried parsley, salt and pepper to taste (2 half-twists from each grinder) and peas from a tin divided three ways.

There had been a brief experiment with broccoli but its lack of uniformity and resistance to being divided up equally meant the peas made a triumphal return to the plate the following week.

The broccoli went the way of celeriac and sweet potatoes, confined to supper time anecdotes told over the comfort of the familiar dish of the day.

Mealtimes were the most obvious window that Lucy had into her parents slide into a life led by habit and ritual.

Cleaning was a full-time occupation for her mother. The collection of cleaning products in the carrier was customised according to the room, and the area declared out of bounds until well after she had exited the room backwards with a final flourish of the vacuum cleaner.

Her reward, a cup of tea and digestive to accompany the satisfaction of a job well done. Lucy once pointed out that most of the rooms were undisturbed between their turns on the cleaning rota, to which her mother replied, 'dust accumulates. It's not a council house you know.'

Which Lucy conceded was accurate, infallible, and completely barmy.

If the house was spotless, and it was, the outside was subjected to its own routine to conquer the elements.

This was her father's territory, a land of neat borders, tidy shed and the 'wilderness' as they jokingly called it, a small fenced off section as far away from the house as possible, where compost and fallen leaves defied order and thus had to be screened from view.

The lawn was trimmed twice a week and the timing of the first and last cut of the season a twice-yearly trigger for much fretting and anxiety.

Friday night dinner with them was Lucy's one concession to living like they did and sticking to a set pattern. Six days a week she was free.

One Friday before Christmas she'd told them she would pop in on the Saturday morning as the office party was scheduled for the Friday.

The party was a bit of a sad affair, with office politics dominating the seating and conversation. A few of them had agreed to call it a night early and secretly meet up in town later, so forgoing the Christmas pudding, slurred speeches and awkward silences she popped in to see them on her way home to change.

After their alarm at the doorbell being rung in the 'middle of the night' (8.27pm) and reassurance that everything was okay, they settled back into their places on matching chairs in front of the TV.

While they speculated over what minor trauma had befallen the cast of Coronation Street in their absence, Lucy went through to put the kettle on and discovered a place had been laid for her in the dining room.

On the kitchen worktop she found an untouched plate of cold salmon, potatoes and peas.

Cooking on the electric hob and in the top oven was a routine so entrenched that Lucy suspected the appliances would follow the same daily habit even if they weren't switched on between Countdown and the News.

Sunday roast was a ceremonial occasion when the bottom oven was allowed its weekly contribution to the family diet. Monday was its day for a thorough clean, and it was allowed the rest of the week off while it's little sibling the top oven took care of the baking and roasting needs.

She said, 'Look at this dear, another gas explosion.'

He said, 'Is that the one in Chippenham I read about?'

She said, 'Yes, I said gas wasn't safe, didn't I?'

He said, 'You did indeed. And I bet

some poor soul in Chippenham wishes they'd listened to you.'

She said, 'I don't know anyone in Chippenham.'

He said, 'But if you did, you'd have warned them about gas. Like you did next door.'

She said, 'That Mr Bartholemew thought he'd save money by converting to gas, but I told him, it's no use having money stashed away when you're blown to kingdom come Mr Bartholemew. Don't you go risking this street. I told him.'

He said, 'You certainly did dear.'

She said, 'And did he thank me?'

He said, 'Do you think there's any more tea in the pot dear?'

She said, 'Not a word. Just stood there shaking his head like one of those what-do-you-call-them?'

He said, 'I'll pour it myself then, shall I?'

She said, 'Those things that shake...'

He said, 'Maracas? Epileptics? Talcum powder?'

She said, 'Don't be daft. Those silly toy dogs, like the one on the parcel shelf of the car at number 42. It must block their view. I bet they have gas. If we all go up, it'll be because of number 42. You mark my words.'

He said, 'Consider them marked dear.'

Lucy recalled a holiday in Norfolk when she was a girl. The chalet had a gas cooker, a new and frightening method of catering to her mother and one which caused so much stress they ate out for most of the week, much to Lucy and her brother's delight.

Routine for them wasn't a choice, it was a gradual slide into consistency that permeated everything in their world.

Even their clothes seemed dull and the house bare of anything that hinted at the passage of time, except for the daily paper, which only reinforced their suspicion of the world beyond their front door.

Along with the 6 o'clock news it served as another barrier to their venturing beyond well-trodden paths to the doctors, supermarket, and every six months an adventure to the dentist.

Lucy's father was a gentle man. A kindly soul they said at his retirement party. A plumber who found work with a paint factory, where the money was less than if he'd worked for himself, but the hours were regular, the work undemanding and the security of work invaluable. He'd met her mother at a factory social evening, when she had been in the typing pool. When that folded, she kept working three days a week as a secretary and together they plodded on contented and happy with Lucy and her brother Neal to occupy their time.

While Lucy settled into the routine of office work, at home she fought against routine with the same ferocity that her parents had adopted it.

Even so she was the safe and dependable one. The one who would check up on them and who had a steady income.

Neal was two years younger than her and from the moment he entered the home he had attacked life with an energy that left those around him exhausted.

In his teenage years he channelled his vitality into a string of bands, playing the guitar with considerably more energy than ability.

One incarnation of his band (they were always his) had a minor hit on local radio. Moscow Blitz picked up some airplay and Neal did an interview for Sounds magazine, which was 40 minutes on the phone and ended up as a four-line entry in the 'ones to watch' section.

Nevertheless, it was a success of sorts, and a proper recording session was arranged with money borrowed from his parents.

It all petered out, band members went to university or got jobs and Neal disappeared.

At first it was a concern but, as his father put it, 'He's always been a boisterous one, probably off with some girl.' Gradually it dawned on Lucy that this wasn't one of his wild weekends and that maybe something had happened.

The police were called, family were told not to worry, enquiries were made, interviews happened, friends questioned, time slipped away.

Days became weeks, his presence hanging around the house like a shadow, tantalisingly out of reach. Gradually the police lost interest, while reassuring the family they hadn't. 'Enquiries are on-going, but he probably got in a spot of bother and is laying low, you know these musician types...'

Routine returned, work, shopping, cleaning, television, sleep, work, shop, clean, tv, sleep, repeat.

When Lucy's father retired it had been 23 years to the day since they'd last seen him. He had never been declared legally dead; an option that had been offered to them more than once. He was gradually set aside and consigned to the untidy cupboard below the bookcase, along with the yellow pages, dog-eared theatre programmes from long ago and photo albums with brittle pages stuck together by time.

Retirement meant a new routine. Neal still grinned from the photo in the tarnished silver frame, but his room was repurposed long ago with little sentiment.

He was still 'missing', probably still slashing at his guitar in Australia or India or somewhere exotic according to his father.

Tonight, being Friday, dinner was the usual salmon, boiled potatoes slightly al-dente, peas.

He said, 'Did I tell you we saw a gas van outside number 42 yesterday?'

She said, 'It's not natural, gas.'

Lucy said, 'I think it is, it comes from under the ground.'

She said, 'That's as maybe, but so do volcanoes and even her at number 42 can't claim they are safe.'

He said, 'I do believe Iceland is powered by volcanoes.'

She said, 'Well, it's a blessing we have a Sainsburys nearby then.'

Lucy said, 'You know I've been having trouble with my neighbours?'

He said, 'Yes dear.'

She said, 'The ones above with the boy?'

Lucy said, 'That's right. She has another one on the way now.'

She said, 'Oh dear. More tea?'

Lucy said, 'Well, I think I'm finally going to have to move.'

She said, 'There's more in the pot. I'll pop the kettle on and refresh it shall I?'

He said, 'That'd be smashing love. Can't beat a good cup of tea eh Lucy?'

Lucy said, 'Well, I was wondering if you'd be able to help. Just a bit. With the money. You know, a loan maybe so I can get somewhere quieter?'

He said, 'We can think about it. Ah, here's mum with that tea.'

Lucy realised this wasn't going any further tonight. She'd been tense but now the subject had been raised she could relax and leave them to think about it.

She took a sip of her tea.

***

The following morning the low sun cast the shadow of the neighbour's fence over the wilderness. Their breath hung in the air as they stood together next to the compost pile. He leaned on a shovel.

He said, 'Next to the Begonias do you think?'

She said, 'Or the border over there.

It's due to be dug over anyway.'

He said, 'That's perfect. She'll be near to her brother, they'll like that.'

She nodded agreement and picked up the garden fork.

Two hours later they shovelled the last of the earth back on and patted it down.

He said, 'Best get a move on, we'll miss the start of Casualty.'

She said, 'You finish up here, I'll pop the kettle on.'

Ray Canham

Thanks be to Len

Len was the sort of man who would have added his pub team's quiz night victory to his CV. If he had ever got around to updating it that is. It was stored on a floppy disc somewhere along with obsolete phone chargers and miscellaneous wires.

He had built a mediocre career with the same haulage company he had been with for most of his adult life, slowly working his way from the loading bay to an administrative job without responsibility for anything more animate than a temperamental photocopier.

Most of his occupation, like the rest of his life, had been unremarkable. A buy-out by another firm left him as one of only three people in the office unaffected. Mostly because no one knew what he did.

That was the nub of his career right there. No one knew what he did, and that included him. He filed a few reports away and looked after the office equipment service contracts but, at a push, that was one day of work a week. Including lunch and coffee breaks.

He spread the few other tasks he had over the week and the rest of the time he pottered around, chatted to people at the coffee station and posted to a nostalgia Facebook group from his mobile, where people with artificial hips and heart bypasses used their mobile phones to convince each other that the world was better in their day.

Len knew the world had been better in 'his day'. He just wasn't sure when that was. He recalled his childhood without enthusiasm. It hadn't been terrible, but his parents constant struggle to meet the rent meant they worked most evenings, his mother at cleaning jobs and his father pulling as much overtime as possible at the factory where he assembled radios.

The house had been littered with the detritus of his father's constant repairs to the family radiogram with parts 'left-over' from work.

Now Len had the nicest council flat in the block. He knew this to be the case because he had received a framed letter, presented by the leader of the council to *'Thank him for having such a well presented and looked after home.'* It had been given to him in an awkward ceremony in the lounge of the adjoining sheltered housing block.

Len had taken Friday off work to attend the lunchtime ceremony. He had bought a new suit from the supermarket, adding a tie and brown striped shirt from the charity shop and shined his shoes with the crumbling remains of polish from the back of the cupboard under the sink.

His speech was written out long hand then condensed onto cards that he could flip through. Nervous all week, he was dressed and ready to go by 10:00 am, three hours before he was due to arrive.

When his name was called, he walked forward, shook the hand proffered by the council leader and was politely ushered away while the recipient of the best kept garden was summoned.

He was home by 2pm; the taste of warm white wine and disappointment kept him company all afternoon. By teatime he had set his speech alight from the gas fire and dropped it in the sink.

By 9pm he had curled up in bed and sobbed himself to sleep. The embers of his foolishness in believing it was something more significant than a photo opportunity for the councillors burned deep within him.

He never let himself get disillusioned again, by simply avoiding anything that might lead to disappointment.

Average. That's how Len described himself. It was the word he used on the one occasion he tried on-line dating.

Average intelligence, average height, average weight, although he conceded perhaps a bit above that these days.

He'd even measured his penis and was pleased to discover it was average in length, although he wasn't sure what allowances he should or shouldn't make for the foreskin, and how much stretching was permissible to get an accurate reading. He hoped quite a bit. He decided not to add that to his profile, unsure of the etiquette of such revelations.

Average. He'd be the first to admit that it didn't bring the flurry of eager singletons to his profile that he'd hoped for.

He pepped it up a bit later but apart from some suspicious Eastern European women, who even Len realised were not in his league, if indeed they existed at all, he only went on one date.

It was with a woman called Jane who barely spoke the whole evening except to say 'I don't mind' in answer to every question and took 2 hours to eat her spaghetti. She left while Len went to the lavatory after settling the bill.

He deleted his profile when he got home.

The local children who hung around on the wall outside his block called him by whatever slur was fashionable in the press at the time; perv, scrounger or fogey.

The taunts were half-hearted at best,

and mostly, he thought, from a sense of duty on their part to ridicule his generation.

He felt for them, bored latch-key kids left to roam, but on the one occasion he'd tried to talk to them he'd been called an effing paedo and his window had been pelted with clods of earth.

He was left alone when a family from Bangladesh moved in nearby and they became the target. Len knew that was unfair on the Khatuns, who seemed very nice and always said hello to him, but he felt relieved all the same and vowed never to try and engage the children again. Once bitten...

He used to attend a weekly quiz night to divide up the working week. Thursday evenings in the Bull. He'd been asked to join a team from work, all of whom had eventually decided that it wasn't for them, although he once played against them in a charity quiz, so he suspected they dropped him and moved on.

His most recent team had been quite formidable and with the right questions and pitted against average teams they did well. Doug was in his 20s, lank hair, denim waistcoat and BO, but he knew a thing or two about sport.

Anita was the barmaid and joined in because she had Thursdays off. She knew all sorts about music and celebrities.

Hamid was a cashier from the local supermarket, didn't drink but liked the quiz nights because, he said, he learnt a lot about Britain. His specialist subject was history, especially British history, about which he knew more than everyone else on the team despite being born in Sri Lanka.

Len's specialist subject was general knowledge.

At school he was above average, a quick learner and eager to please. It drew him to the attention of his tutors, who gave him assignments to stretch his knowledge, and to his classmates, who singled him out for being the teachers' pet.

By the time he reached secondary school he was taking refuge in mediocrity. Too much or too little effort brought unwanted attention but coasting along kept him secure and under the radar.

50 years after leaving school with 5 GCSEs, the exact amount an average pupil was expected to get at the time, he retired.

The suit almost fitted him, without the need for the faux leather belt that came with it, and the shirt had been replaced by a nice lilac one with matching tie from a supermarket.

His retirement speech went down well, even if his manager had cut it short by leading the clapping after a rather poor joke and declared him a good fellow, wished him a very happy retirement, told him not to be a stranger and gave him the rest of the cake in a paper bag to take home.

**

At first retirement wasn't too difficult. He was good at pottering and making simple tasks stretch through the day. But after a diet of too much daytime TV and his quiz team folding, he decided he needed a hobby.

When it came, it wasn't what he, or anyone who knew him, expected.

His Thursday evening at the pub was a habit he found hard to break. Anita was usually there, and the others would drop in with decreasing frequency. Quiz nights had been replaced by band nights and one Thursday evening Len held the door open for a young man carrying an amplifier that looked like it was held together by stickers.

From the clientele already assembled around the bar and the look of the band setting up, Len soon reached the conclusion that whatever was going to happen, it wasn't going to be to his tastes.

Where music was concerned Len had, predictably, always favoured middle-of-the-road stuff, veering towards Country.

Rusty Razörz was scrawled on the drumkit, although Len couldn't help noticing the bands logo was squashed as it reached the right edge, to the point where the r and z were merged and smaller than the rest of the lettering.

Amateurs, he thought to himself as he carried his pint to a table as far back from the offcut of carpet that was doing duty as the stage as he could get.

'You a fan then, or dad of one of em?' A young woman asked as she carefully positioned three pints of Guinness on the table.

'Never heard of them, just here for a swift pint. I don't think it's quite my scene,' he replied.

The girl shrugged and supped at a pint, leaving her with a white moustache which she wiped away with the back of a black lace glove.

'They are pretty good, featured in Sounds last week. That's a music paper.'

'Like the Melody Maker?'

'Yeah, but less crap.'

'I see. Well, thank you. I think I'll give it a miss.'

And Len did intend to give it a miss. He listened politely as the band were introduced to a few half-hearted cheers, and then winced into his beer as a wail of feedback, discordant strumming and tapping of microphones indicated they were getting ready.

'Ello muppets, we're Rusty Razörz, 1, 2, 3, 4, let's gooooo!'

Len got as far as the inner door when a wall of sound hit him. It was as much physical as it was musical. He felt it in his bones, a wave of sound, but more than that, it was visceral, almost alive.

As one song blurred into another, all at a breakneck pace, he was transfixed.

Back home reflecting on the evening, ears still ringing, Len understood that it wasn't about the music, or even being able to play it well. It was the whole nerve shredding experience.

He'd found something, although he wasn't sure what it was.

He had watched from the back, leant against the wall with the remains of his pint untouched, standing with people who just accepted him.

He saw a poster advertising another appearance by Rusty Razörz, so out of curiosity he went along.

He also caught two other bands on the bill and again came home with the curious sensation of not quite understanding what he'd witnessed, but knowing that he loved it.

Len became a regular on the scene, a nodding acquaintance to punks in studded leather, whippet thin skater types with dreads, but mostly with ordinary young people, whose uniform seemed to be the avoidance of uniforms.

***

It was on a Saturday at the Maypole, an out-of-town pub known more for folk music than punk, that Len's life really changed.

The landlord's son had suggested the mini festival. A combination of parental indulgence and the promise of heavy afternoon drinking swelling the tills convinced them to give it a try.

It all went well. Len could now discern different styles and nuances, knew the run-of-the-mill to the truly original and was, as ever, gratified and inspired by the spirit of cooperation among the bands.

Apart from a willingness to share equipment and instruments, several musicians would pop up in different bands, sometimes as a late substitute for a missing member, often because they played in lots of bands just for the thrill of it.

Len chatted to a man who introduced

himself as Robbo. He played bass guitar with one band, guitar with a different one and sang and played guitar with yet another.

By the end of the evening, he still wasn't sure of the sequence of events or quite how the conversation went, but Len had evidently promised to help finance a record from his pension.

Thus, the first release by Vortex IV was also the first to bare the legend *'Thanks be to Len'* next to a stylised picture featuring Len on the label.

Vortex IV was followed by Marine-Gun, another Vortex IV 7-inch, and his first album, a compilation of local bands.

Mr Khatun told his wife he thought retirement suited Len. He always seemed to be busy and looked younger, with a spring in his step.

The Khatun's son was learning guitar at an after-school club, with instruments donated by local bands, an initiative set up by Len, although his involvement was in the strictest confidence.

Len had found his hobby and, he reflected, a life. He was regarded as a friend to the bands and their followers and even been interviewed for a local fanzine, an awkward affair that served to further his status as the mysterious man behind the scenes.

"At home I'm a Jim Reeves guy, but I want to let these bands have a chance. I like to hear them play live.
I give them a few bob, and they make a record."

Most of the time he was repaid. But apart from almost never having to buy his own drink, which the bands soon realised was only ever a pint, maybe a second if it was an all-dayer, he never made any profit, and even lost a bit on the albums. All of which he thought was a small price to pay.

The local children left him alone now, after Suicide Suzie, 5ft 7 inches of spiky hair and hormonal rage had a word with them in her inimitable style.

Len was preparing for his 14th release, a live recording of Rusty Razörz, when the letter arrived. He put it to one side and continued putting a cheque made out to the pressing plant in a file along with his notes and put it carefully back in the drawer.

After studiously filling in the cheque stub, he made plans to hand it over to one of the band on Monday, when he had been invited to sit in on the recording session.

When he had finished he opened and read the letter, turned it over and read the back, which seemed to be a long list of ways to pay the bill itemised on the other side.

That HMRC wanted a share of his profits was understandable, if unwelcome.

The fact that he'd not made any money didn't seem to occur to them, but that was secondary to the fine that they were demanding because he'd not registered as self-employed or filed any paperwork.

He had a dim recollection of reading their previous correspondence, but as he was losing money, breaking even at best, he'd assumed it wasn't necessary for him to do anything.

This letter was a demand for money with the threat of extra fines if it wasn't paid promptly, so after a sleepless night and frightened that he'd lose his flat, he employed a solicitor to sort it out for him.

A few gigs and the launch of the Rusty Razörz album at a packed and emotional town hall re-energised him.

The solicitor assured him that everything had been sorted out and he was now free to carry on as before, but, and he emphasised this by going over it twice during their meeting and once more as he ushered him out through the waiting room and into the rain beyond, 'You must keep a record and signed receipt of every donation and subsequent payment.'

Which just left Len with a hefty solicitors' bill.

And no way to pay it.

The Rusty Razörz album was raising money for an anti-racism campaign group, so Len hadn't asked for his investment back.

At the time he'd been happy to help, life wasn't exactly hand to mouth with his company pension topped up by a state one. He was doing okay and had a little put aside with which to fund the album, but now he felt the world was closing in on him.

He had drifted through most of his life, smoothing the ups and downs to gentle ripples. He had found excitement and purpose late in life but now he felt foolish and alone.

After missing a couple of gigs he was expected at, he took a call from Alan, guitarist with Vortex IV. He said they'd missed him and just wanted to make sure he was okay. Len told him he was 'just a bit weary' and thanked him for calling.

That night Len reflected that when he was off sick from the haulage firm for a fortnight with shingles he was never contacted at home.

As he remembered it, going back to work was just like any other Monday. No one asked him how he'd been, and he suspected only the HR manager he'd called to report in sick knew had been away.

He pondered on the comradery of the scene he'd joined and been welcomed into. He, Mr Average, had been taken in by a subculture and was, possibly for the first time as an adult, missed by someone. He wept, whether from sadness or happiness he wasn't sure.

Dragging himself along the next time Vortex IV played in The Bull, he was still experiencing mixed emotions when he went in, but the backslapping, cheery waves, 'hellos' and 'how are yous?' and the nod from across the room from Suicide Suzy, caught him unawares and he found himself at the bar with a tear in his eye.

**

Three weeks later, after Alan had got the full story from him, Len was seated on a bench at the back of the Maypole.

A hastily assembled collection of local bands, and some not so local, had been recruited and *'Len Aid'*, subtitled *'f*ck solicitors'* on some posters, was underway.

Members of some well-known bands had shown up and Len was introduced to a succession of people he would only recognise again by their tattoos, and to a producer who'd 'done things with Stiff Little Fingers,' who Alan hastily explained had been an influential band from Belfast, after seeing the bemused look on Len's face.

Len had to admit he'd never heard of The Substrates either, but he was assured they had been quite the 'thing' on the scene and the fact that three of them were doing an acoustic set impressed everyone else there.

They finished with a raucous version of Jim Reeve's Distant Drums in honour of Len, with enthusiastic backing vocals provided by Suicide Suzie.

It was the best day's takings ever at the Maypole.

Vortex IV headlined, and before what he described as the carefully choreographed spontaneous encore, Robbo announced that they'd raised enough money to pay off Len's legal bills and there was some left over to donate to the childrens music club.

He raised a pint glass from the stage and as one the crowd turned to Len with drinks aloft.

***

The heart attack was massive. It took people a while to realise the slumped figure alone at the back of the field was Len, and he hadn't just nodded off.

The last day of his average life was the happiest day Len had ever had.

Ray Canham

The Savage

London, 1958

I'd always wondered what could drive a person to take a life. What motivates someone to look another in the eye and end their existence? To deny them everything. No more sunrises or sunsets, no more Christmas holidays with the family, the smell of pine and roast meat, the squeal of toddlers high on sugar and excitement. The chance to hug children or grandchildren, to stare into an ocean. To dance, sing and to fall in love.

Soldiers do it of course, but there is a contract there of sorts, and we could probably all kill if we or our loved ones were threatened.

Revenge? Maybe, although thinking and planning it is one thing, but to carry out the act itself, to watch the light dim and go out in someone's eyes, that's different.

Mad, an animal, a monster, a savage? Today they'd use the word sociopath. They're all excuses, names given to separate them from us. But are we so different?

My father wasn't any of those things. Not really. He was a gentle man who had played the tea chest bass in a skiffle band and kept an immaculate caravan in Tenby where we'd all decamp during the summer holidays.

He was in the army during the war. He entered service in 1943 as a gunner on an army launch ferrying troops, until an unfortunate incident, that I only learned about much later, and not from him. Following orders, he had fired on an Italian boat and taken three lives.

An enquiry established they were Maquis; French resistance fighters being brought ashore.

No blame was attached to him or the skipper, but he ended up on desk duty and found himself in Germany as the war ended. Not quite a broken man but certainly more sober.

After the war he found work as a clerk in a department store, five days a week, 08:30 to 17:30.

He taught me to play chess in the evenings, and on a Saturday, took my sister to her riding lessons, where he'd sit in his Austin 40 and read the paper.

When she was done, he'd drop her at home, kiss my mum on the cheek as she handed him a packed lunch wrapped in greaseproof paper, and head off to watch the football.

West Ham was his team, and he was a season ticket holder. If they were playing away, he'd go to Georgio's Milk Bar in the shadow of Upton Park where the loyal fans would gather to listen to the scores on the wireless.

On Saturday evenings he'd take my mother out dancing or to the pictures.

Occasionally these were family affairs but mostly my sister and I would stay home and listen to the wireless; Saturday Skiffle Club and Talk of the Town followed by A Book at Bedtime.

Sunday morning, he would walk to the drafty pre-fab Methodist chapel on Barking Road. The original chapel had been bombed during the war and my father sat on the committee that was trying to get a permanent replacement.

Meanwhile my mother would practice her own devotion, to her first love, English Literature.

Our bookshelves overflowed with the classics, a treasure trove for the scholar my mother had been, and my sister was aiming for. Hardy, Dickens, the Bronte sisters, Eliot and Austin rubbing shoulders with my father's collection of gramophone records and lever arch files of sheet music.

He was no mean pianist, but mother was the one for the upright piano in the hallway, entertaining us with singalongs, marching tunes which my sister and I would stomp about the house to, and at Christmas, carols.

If the weather was fine, and I recall it often was, we'd go out in the Austin and 'take in the air' somewhere in the country.

In the winter, and on wet summer days, we'd visit elderly relatives. Granny puff-puff, who smoked like a chimney and would cough up lungfuls of phlegm into a hanky mid conversation, then carry on as if nothing had happened.

Or Aunt Doris, a nervous, stick thin lady who always sat on a dining chair, back stiff as a board, knees together and a cup and saucer rattling on her lap. She'd never been the same after next door was bombed out.

Doris had been with her mother in the Anderson Shelter in their back garden. Rubble from the blast covered the shelter and trapped the family inside.

It wasn't until her mother didn't turn up for work at the grocers 12 hours later that her boss sent the delivery boy round to check on her.

Then there was Uncle Fred, a lively old man, with a yellow pallor and great big hands with liver spots.

He'd laugh and tell me he had his own

map of the tube on his left hand, then he'd pick out the stations, Bow, Mile End, change here by the knuckle for the Central Line, Stepney, Whitechapel, that one up there, that's Stratford and then right up here, he'd trace an imaginary line up his little finger to a scar just below the nail, that's Leyton. 'You don't want to go there son,' he'd say, a big grin spreading across his face.

Very occasionally I'd be permitted to accompany my mother on one of her infrequent visits to her uncle Nigel in Hove. The train ride was exciting and the seaside a treat.

Nigel lived in a gorgeous art deco flat 200 yards from the promenade. It faced a neat public garden and across the way an identical terrace of flats.

It felt like an entirely different world, which in many ways it was. My father never visited. He'd drop us at the station, wind down the window, call me back, press a shilling into my hand 'for the pier' and tell me to be careful, and with a wink to my mother, say, 'Don't go catching queer lad.'

Nigel lived with Rupert, who had been a theatre director in London and moved south, 'to bring a little culture to the provinces dear...'.

I'm not sure if Brighton and Hove

were ever the cultural wasteland he made them out to be, but Nigel quickly found a kindred spirit in Rupert.

Nigel had been a teacher, but rumours about his private life started to intrude and despite assurances from the head teacher, he was, or thought he was, under constant suspicion.

Eventually an anonymous letter found its way onto the headmaster's desk demanding that, *'The mathematics tutor be removed with immediate effect, or the press shall be made aware that you are harbouring a monster who indulges in unnatural acts...'*

He lost his job. Private tutoring brought in a little income, but meeting Rupert, who already owned the flat and kept a small apartment in London for 'business and recreation' was his way out of his dingy room in the boarding house.

Once a month we'd all cram into the Austin and make the trek to mum's sister Celia in Harrow.

She was the other black sheep in our family according to my parents. Celia maintained she and Nigel were the only white sheep amongst a family of black ones.

She had married a man called Maurice, a Jewish tailor who owned a shop on Pinner High Road.

The problem wasn't his job or

religion, it was that he'd been arrested three times for taking part in protests against Mosley's black shirts and his fascist party.

Maurice died in 1949, a heart attack my mother swore was from too much agitation and being mixed up with anarchists and 'the wrong sort'.

Celia was by then an active member of the Communist Party, proclaiming international socialism and equality for all workers, while bathed in the light cast by the William Morris-stained glass window on the stairwell of her three-bed semi in leafy Harrow.

'Not the British way,' my father would pronounce over the top of the Daily Herald, which he took along as a barrier to making conversation with Celia.

Maurice's 'livelier' exploits were always discussed, despite warnings to the contrary on the way over. I admit I was often the one to raise them.

To me Maurice was a hero, a swashbuckling gentleman, always well turned out but ready for a punch-up, which in my mind was a bout of Queensbury rules fisticuffs between two or maybe three adversaries while their chums looked on, just like our heroes in the Saturday morning cinema club.

I romanticised him and his daring deeds and Celia did nothing to dissuade me, indeed I think she overlooked the savagery of street fighting too and idolised her memory of the suave freedom fighter coming home bloodied in a torn suit with a summons to appear before the magistrate.

We always left before dinner because father was strictly a meat and two veg man and Celia preferred what my mother called, 'exotic foreign nonsense.'

I'd usually find a book and selection of pamphlets in my satchel when I got home, secreted there by Celia on one of her frequent trips to the cloakroom, '...because of her unnatural diet, too much spice and grains,' according to my father.

Celia's recommended reading material was strictly forbidden in our household, so our tacit arrangement meant late night reading by torchlight.

I got a good grounding in Communism, Atheism, Marx, Freud, and all manner of anti-fascist literature thanks to her.

Oh, and my father had assisted the principal executioner, Albert Pierrepoint, at Hameln prison in the British controlled sector of Germany from 1945 up until the end of his military service in 1948.

After being de-mobbed he remained

on the Home Office books as an official executioner.

I remember him collecting his travelling case, trilby, umbrella and a packed lunch from the telephone stand in the hall before heading for the station on these infrequent appointments.

He wore solemn clothing and a serious expression.

The following evening he'd come home £6.10 shillings richer and clutching his receipts for the journey.

A fortnight later a cheque would be delivered for the other half of his fee and his expenses. He'd seat himself at his desk after supper and check the amount against the entries in his little logbook, carefully licking the end of his pencil and drawing a ruled line under each entry once he was satisfied the state hadn't cheated him out of his fare and meal allowance.

His occasional nights away weren't ever discussed and I'm not quite sure how I knew what he was doing.

The household was always tense the day before he left and sombre the night he arrived home.

One time he returned with a doll for my sister, a colouring book and paints for me and some flowers for mother.

I stormed into the kitchen to get a jar

of water for my paints and found him and mother holding hands across the table. I heard him say it didn't go as planned, then, seeing me, he forced a smile and said, 'Hello champ, let's find you a jar,' as he bent down to forage under the sink for a suitable receptacle.

***

I had just turned 14 years old when my mother asked me to deliver some papers to Celia, on the other side of the city.

I could do it all on the Metropolitan line, with a bit of forward planning and if I timed it right could avoid getting lost in the warren of platforms and lines at Baker Street interchange.

Celia had been given strict instructions to meet me at Harrow-on-the Hill station.

I was issued with two pennies for the phone box should anything go amiss and a set of directions from the station to Celia's house, 'just in case, you know what a mop head she can be...', her telephone number and ours, instructions on what platforms to get on for the return journey and even a complicated hand drawn map of Baker Street Underground interchange in case of the unforeseen need to change trains.

Armed with so much responsibility I

set off on my adventure from Plastow station full of excitement.

I was bored by the time we reached Euston Square, then all a flutter as we pulled out of Baker Street until the welcome sight of Finchley Road confirmed I was on the right branch.

I relaxed a bit, but stood up as soon as we departed Northwick Park and hung onto an overhead strap, swaying with the movement of the train, until, at last, we pulled in and I stepped onto the platform at Harrow-on-the-Hill and into the waiting arms of Celia.

I handed her the envelope, apparently some family records she needed to make an insurance claim. Having asked I was none the wiser.

I let myself be led to her house where the promise of a Chinese style luncheon awaited. Out of the station onto Lowlands Road, left along Bessborough Road, where some shops were still boarded up and unoccupied due to bomb damage in the war, over at the crossing, down through the Avenues, tidy houses set back from the road where Celia pointed out the saplings supported by stakes.

She told me the original trees had been removed by well-meaning locals and intended for the war effort, but by the time they were seasoned and ready to use I'd be a grown man. We turned right into Whitmore Road and Celia's nice house.

We had just stepped inside, where I was sitting on a stool untying my laces, when the first brick shattered the window of the front parlour.

Celia cursed as she burst past me, and flung open the door, just as the second brick went through the lounge window.

The man with the jerry can and lighted newspaper on the doorstep was as startled as she was to find him there.

They both seemed to freeze while I tugged my shoe back on and stood up.

Then everything happened at once, as if time was trying to catch up with itself. The man who'd thrown the bricks was shouting, calling Celia a 'commie bitch' and Celia was calling them both fascist scum.

The second man was already sprinting away down the road yelling curses about Jews and commies behind him. The man holding the jerry can flung the newspaper and made to run off, but as he turned, Celia yanked his collar and dragged him to the ground.

She was beating him with clenched fists, but Aunt Celia was no street fighter and he quickly rolled on top of her, saying something to her through gritted teeth as he pinned her down.

It was stupid really, looking back, but my reaction was instantaneous. Celia screamed as I flew out of the doorway and launched myself at him, the height of the doorstep giving me extra momentum.

I had no idea what would happen next. I expected a good pummelling, but it was Aunt Celia's concrete Buddha that saved me.

Celia's assailant struck his head against it with such force that the sound of his skull cracking lives with me still. He lay there as I stooped over him, mesmerised by the blood coming from his head and pooling at the Buddha's feet.

Even now it's all in slow motion in my memory. He seemed to be coming round, making indistinct noises. I was leaning over him, taking in the little scar on his temple, the downy stubble on his chin, his dirty collar, and his eyes, grey under heavy eyelids and thick eyebrows.

His lips were turning blue as the blood flowed out. I pressed my hand to the wound to try and stop the bleeding.

Somewhere a million miles away I heard Celia struggling to get up and sliding on the gravel drive. I pressed hard but to no avail. I watched as the life ebbed out of him.

Limp, shaking and numb, I was led

into the kitchen. Celia disappeared for a few minutes then returned, having, I later found out, dragged the body into the begonias.

She led me to the bathroom and tenderly washed my hands, murmuring soothing words. She made me a cup of sweet tea, then sat in the hallway making a series of telephone calls.

She returned, pulled up a stool opposite me and lifted my chin so our eyes met. She told me Maurice had lots of chums who could help, mostly former members of the 43 group who'd led the fightback against Mosley's black shirts. Soon a man would call round who could help, and it would be okay, but there were things to do.

An hour or so later a white window cleaners van pulled up on the driveway, then a little Austin like my fathers.

The 'window cleaners' made busy in the garden. 'They need to put on a show for the neighbours, so once they have our friend in the van, I get my windows cleaned. Not such a bad day after all.' She smiled but I knew it was for show.

Howard, a gruff old man with curly white hair, round spectacles and long unruly eyebrows that made him look like an owl, walked in and sat beside me at the kitchen table.

'This the lad?' He asked Celia. 'Well, it's not what we wanted but it's done. Let's go now.'

With that I was whisked from Celia's embrace and made to lay under a blanket on the back seat of the Austin. After a while we stopped and I heard another man get in, a shushed conversation and we were off.

Occasionally Howard would ask if I was okay but that was as far as communication went until we pulled up in the yard behind a clothes factory. Howard led me inside. I was still dazed, but although he was firm, he seemed kind.

He took me into a little office with files everywhere and bits of cloth hanging on a line overhead. He sat me in a comfortable chair next to a stove, where a kettle was already whistling away on top.

A old woman came in and fussed over me, making more sweet tea, trying to give me sweets and pastries. I wasn't hungry but nibbled away to keep her happy.

I never knew her name, apart from Howard no one was introduced and amongst themselves no names were ever used. The kind woman and Howard were bickering constantly, about where I should go, who with, about who was to blame and then, like a bolt out of the blue she asked him about my parents.

I'd not thought of them until then. All the shame and their horror when they found out their son was a murderer welled up and that's when I broke down.

The woman hugged me as I shook and sobbed uncontrollably, rocking with me and making gentle shushing noises, whispering 'it's okay, it's okay.'

Howard berated her, 'Look what you've done, I had him under control.' I heard him say.

'He's just a boy, let him be for now. You'll be okay lad, you're among friends now.' I said I was sorry, kept repeating it.

'Hey boy...' This was from Howard. 'You did a man's work today. Foolish, dangerous and a blooming mess to clear up, but never be sorry for what you did. You defended your auntie and boy, look at me boy...now stop with the kvetching, you're a man now, we'll see you right.'

I spent the night in that office. I was assured my parents would be told by Celia that I was staying the night with her.

They told me I had to be out of the office 'before the girls come in on Monday morning,' so Sunday, after a lunch of bagel and salmon, something I'd never tried before, I was back under the blanket in my first ever suit that the kind lady had found for me, my hair trimmed and a kippah on my head.

Howard wore one too, and told me I was to be his nephew, taking the air in Brighton. We'd be getting the train from Waterloo and 'arrangements had been made' from there.

The journey was uneventful, and with none of the excitement I usually felt travelling on this line. In Brighton we had tea in a small café on a back street near the station.

Howard approached the owner; words were exchanged, and we were whisked out the back. An hour later, Howard pointed me towards the seafront and told me to 'walk, turn right at the promenade and keep the sea on your left, and you'll meet someone who'll help'.

He wished me 'Shalom,' and darted back into the café, closing the door behind him.

The promenade was familiar but not as familiar as the voice that hailed me from a shelter as I walked past.

'Ho there my boy, come hither and keep your uncle Nigel company.'

I joined him, assuming it was a chance meeting. I told him I was in trouble and not to get mixed up. He said he knew and went on to explain that the Jews and 'his sort' had a lot in common, mostly as targets of the fascists, and the police.

He told me of an underground network to move people around and out of trouble when the local police showed too much interest, or they'd done something for the cause and needed to lay low.

'We have a few West Indians moving about now, some of the cities are a powder keg because of Mosley's crowd.

'Mind you, they are a bit harder to disguise,' he said, grinning. I smiled back and he patted me on the shoulder, 'good lad, let's go.'

Later that year Notting Hill would erupt into race riots. Now, as Nigel had said, tensions were simmering. Homosexuality was illegal and the Jewish community, memories of the dreadful things done to them by the Nazis still fresh, were the targets, not just of fascists but in the mainstream too, after British soldiers were hanged by Zionists in Palestine.

I remember my father cursing at the wireless when the news broke. 'I suppose your sister is celebrating with her red chums,' he said to my mother.

We didn't go to Nigel's flat but met Rupert in a teahouse. He greeted me with sad eyes and a nervy hug.

'I'm so sorry, it must be hell. But fret not, we've got you a ticket on the fairy express, a majestic journey to the wonderous delights of...' he paused, 'Wolverhampton. Maybe not so much delights as... help me out here Nigel love. What does Wolverhampton have to offer?'

Nigel shrugged. Rupert smiled ruefully then snapped his fingers and grinned like a cheshire cat.

'I know, Wolverhampton's sole delight is Miss Deloris Prettyman and her charming guesthouse. All the doilies you can eat, the anti-mascaras have their own tiny anti-mascaras, more lace than you'd think possible and don't get me started on the frills.'

They took me to a posh department store where I was whisked away by a man with a hanky in his top pocket and a tie with the widest knot I'd ever seen. He stared at me with a finger on his chin, put me in a cubicle and came back with a new suit.

This one was much heavier, the collar scratched my neck, and the trousers and sleeves were stiff. He said I'd soon break it in and handed me a shirt and three collars.

As we walked away, I asked them about Celia. They said she was fine. A bit shaken but she could handle herself.

Then I asked about my parents and sister. Weren't they missing me, when could I see them again, when could I go back home?

'Honestly,' Nigel said, 'we don't know. It's out of our hands and the fewer people who know the better.' He went on to explain that Celia knew people who'd sort it.

I was bundled onto a bus that evening with a ticket, a cheese sandwich wrapped in paper and tied with ribbon, £2.00 from Nigel and a set of instructions to the guest house.

I tried to sleep on the bus, but my mind was running at 100 miles an hour. I thought about the life I'd taken, that man, a boy really, not much older than me. What about his family, did he have a sister like I did? Why was he so angry with Celia, just because she wanted a better world without all the hate? But I was the one who'd killed someone, not him.

I thought about the police, were they chasing me? Was my father going to have to decline his stipend from the government, because you couldn't execute your own son, could you?

I must have nodded off because I was shaken awake by the bus jerking to a halt at a bus station.

'Wolverhampton.' The driver called out, and three of us got off. It was 5am.

I followed the instructions I'd been

given, although it took me three attempts to work out which way I had to go from the station.

Victoria Street, where Povey's Café was already open, it's windows steamed up, the clattering of cups and plates reaching me as a bus conductor came out chewing the remains of his breakfast; onto Worchester Road then right to Lea Road, past the allotments and towards Penn Fields, turn right into the alley next to number 74, and then knock on the back door.

That's how I ended up with Deloris. She let three rooms. I had one, all expenses paid apparently, but I was expected to fetch the coal in, chop the kindling and do other odd jobs.

The other rooms were let to people appearing at the local theatres and clubs. A couple of nights after I arrived an elderly man called round and took me into the kitchen, which was where Deloris had her sanctuary away from her guests.

At the long kitchen table, hastily covered with an off-white tablecloth, she sat a cup of tea in front of both of us and made herself scarce.

He introduced himself as Mr French, although even at 14 years old I knew this was a pseudonym.

Obviously used to giving commands he told me that no one would know what I'd done; I'd been a 'klutz' but Celia had assured him that I'd been defending her, and although the future was a bit rocky, I'd be home soon.

I asked about the police, and he assured me they were dealing with things, and that I'd be protected.

He passed on a letter from my parents. It was full of questions, of course, and my father expressed his 'sincerest disappointment that I'd got involved in some ill advised communist stunt.'

Apparently, they'd had a frightful row with Nigel and another with Celia, who was now 'persona non grata' for leading me astray.

A hastily written note from Nigel accompanying their letter explained the cover story; I was in Hove because I'd been at a demonstration with Celia and got in a spot of bother, not my fault etcetera etcetera, and was resting while everyone cooled down. Rupert and Nigel didn't possess their own telephone so I couldn't call.

Even though I knew it was a flimsy story I hoped the version relayed to my parents would convince them, but I had my doubts.

I settled in and was kept busy with errands and my chores. A week after I'd arrived a man called while Deloris was out getting bread.

He was called Peter and sat in the parlour and told me awful jokes, then he got a puppet out of its case to show me how it worked and then gave me two tickets for the show he was in.

When Deloris came home, she greeted him like an old friend and told me to run his cases up to room 2. He insisted on keeping Bobby in his case with him.

I never had the opportunity to go and see the show. Two days later, the day of the show, I was whisked away by Mr French and dropped at the bus terminal.

He handed me a bus ticket for Birmingham, where I was to get the train to London, then he produced a ticket for the train and told me to be polite and to not talk to anyone unless strictly necessary.

All through the bus journey I fretted about making the connection, but I found my platform, took a seat and stared out of the window as the Midlands charged by and villages became towns that became London, where I was met by Celia.

I didn't know how I'd feel about seeing Celia again.

I'd been troubled by dreams of the

dying man, the man I'd killed, and if I had a moment to myself, I'd think about it, about what I'd do differently.

Some days it didn't seem real. Deloris had seemed to understand these moments and would gently steer me in the direction of my next job and start up a conversation about nothing.

Celia ran and hugged me before I'd even stepped down from the carriage. We both sobbed, then talked in staccato bursts, then sobbed again.

She lifted my chin with her hand and looked into my eyes.

'It's all okay, everything is fine.' She said.

It was an awkward few weeks. Celia and my parents didn't speak for ages. I was grounded and told, in no uncertain terms, to grow up and 'not get involved with these communists and yids because no good will come of it.'

Every evening a lecture; My school grades would suffer, I'd not get a decent job, what of my poor mother, or father, depending on whose turn it was to deliver the lesson.

I was still dealing with my own guilt and emotions too, which, thanks to Celia and Nigel's excommunication from the family, I had to keep bottled up.

The end of the summer holidays came too soon, and I went back to school feeling more grown up. I was allowed long trousers and a new satchel.

My experiences over the holidays hardened me. Schoolyard games seemed childish and many of my old friends were just silly children to me.

All the things I'd enjoyed before seemed trivial. I started talking to girls, but arrangements to meet had to be in school time as I was still grounded.

Only the usual family visits were allowed; Gran (no more childish Granny puff-puff nonsense), Aunt Doris, who was as stiff as ever and then Uncle Fred, who I think sensed the change in me and took me aside to ask if I was okay.

I nodded but he knew something was up. He told me about his time as a prisoner of war, how he was interned in Singapore where he had been working as an administrator when the 'Japs' invaded. 'That's why I'm this fetching shade of yellow.' he said, 'Jaundice, but that wasn't the worst of it.'

We were interrupted before he went on. He winked at me as my mother dragged me away to help put his shopping away.

One Thursday Celia surprised me coming out of school. She took my arm and pulled me into the alley beside the railway cutting.

I was full of questions to which she had faltering answers. No, the police weren't involved, the fascists were leaving her alone, she was fine thank you, and still a communist.

I pushed and pushed, particularly about the lack of follow-up and why the police hadn't arrested her, or me.

I still loved Celia but a bit of me was angry with her too, I knew she'd got me to safety, but I was living with so many unknowns and unresolved issues, with guilt and uncertainty.

I was still crossing the street or dodging down a side road when I saw a policeman and never went home past the crossroads on the Barking Road where the police directed traffic.

I took my pent-up anger out on Celia in that dank cutting that smelled of wee, soot and mown grass.

Tears of rage and sadness, but most of all the confusion still hovering over me like a cloud. She tried to hug me, but I fought her off and shouted some stupid things at her.

I said I'd been betrayed, and I was a man now after everything that had happened and I deserved to know the truth, to get some answers so I could settle my mind.

She held me at arm's length, hands on my shoulders, head tilted to one side, then the other, took a deep breath and told me to do the same.

'Okay,' she said. 'If you really want to know, if you really think it'll help.'

She told me.

***

Celia's prominence in the communist party had made her a target for the black shirts, the fascists of Mosley's party.

For a while they had the upper hand at the street demos and party meetings. They had a network of public houses friendly to their cause with back rooms for meetings and out-of-the-way houses owned by prominent leaders for planning their election campaigns.

The disruption that the Communists, along with a re-kindled Jewish resistance modelled on the 43 group, and other anti-fascist activist groups relied upon, was frustrated by a lack of inside information.

A young Communist, Frank Cappello, was therefore planted in with the fascists. His role was to gain their trust and feed information back to his handler, Howard.

He was one of a three-person gang who had attacked Celia's house that day...

As she was telling me I could feel the ground opening, my legs wobbled, my calf muscles went into spasm as I sat back, head in hands.

The chap with him, Warren Bently and the other in a car waiting around the corner, were both paid up Nazis and known troublemakers.

The car driver was never apprehended, but Warren was picked up the following day while having tea with his parents in their semi in Croydon.

'So, I killed the wrong one?'

As I said it, I knew how pathetic that sounded. Celia nodded as she crouched down in front of me.

'Taking a life is never right, but Maurice taught me that sometimes doing the right thing isn't enough.

'I'm so sorry. Frank was a courageous man and knew of the dangers. It was an accident, and you were brave in defending me, you weren't to know.'

I couldn't look her in the eye. I sat trembling, shivering on a warm afternoon.

A train rattled by, then another going in the opposite direction.

'Come on, let's get you a cuppa.' With that Celia hauled me up and led me out of the alley.

She took me to a café on the Uxbridge Road, where we sat me down outside and ordered two teas, with lots of sugar.

1961

Life had returned to something approaching normality. I flunked school, fought with my father over careers and ended up as a 17-year-old stagehand and general dogs-body at The Grand, Wolverhampton.

Officially it was Celia who called in a favour, my parents didn't know I'd been there already. Deloris put me up in my old room off the scullery for a nominal rent plus my chores.

Peter was lodged with Deloris. He was in rehearsals for Cinderella, where he was one of the ugly sisters, his puppet Bobby was the other one.

Every so often we would share the bus home. Sometimes he still had some rouge on, slap we call it in 'the trade'.

Next door to him was Bert Entwistle, who looked like a down at heel salesman but had been half of a comedy double act.

His partner made it big in films, while Bert was reduced to playing the Mayor of

Pumpkinville in Cinderella in Wolverhampton.

I thought both Peter and Bert were rather sad, but on stage they came alive, Bert standing there taking all the abuse and feeding lines. Peter chatting to the front row, throwing sweets into the stalls and making everyone giggle with Bobby's antics.

I used to watch from the wings, marvelling at the way the actors transformed. I saw in them, underneath the garish costumes and outrageous make up, something of my own act. The front I put on to mask the turmoil I felt inside.

Back home my father had been a tad melancholy in the run up to Christmas but was coming out of his funk and had taken the family skating at Alexandra Palace.

This was my mother's assessment in her letter inviting me to join them for 'as long as you can be spared' over the festive period.

She wrote that Father had been away on one of his 'overnighters in the middle of December'. It was only to Pentonville, but he had to be ready for dawn, so he stayed at the Star and Garter over the road and went in at 4am, weaving through the early protesters trying to get their candles to light in the breeze.

There was more, much more. News about Aunt Doris and her nerves, Gran was in and out of hospital 'for her lungs,' and might be in over Christmas, Uncle Fred came second in the Crib league for his Legion Club and then won half a ham in the Christmas raffle.

No mention of Nigel or Celia.

A note was included from my sister. Her letter was short, terse and to the point.

'Come home for Xmas jughead, bring me a present. Dad says don't turn into 'one of them.' I have a boyfriend.

'Love sis. X'

***

I went home on Christmas Eve 1961. It was the lull before panto season kicked off and I had three days free.

Deloris was arranging a little Christmas dinner for Peter and Bert. Before I left, she asked me if she should set a place for Bobby?'

I scoffed as I picked up my bag and unlatched the door, then, turning back I said, 'why not, I'm sure Peter would appreciate the gesture.'

Home was just as I expected it. Paper chains hung around the room, a spindly tree hiding under tinsel and baubles, and a holly wreath on the front door.

Carols were playing on the gramophone, the house was awash with steam, cooking smells and excitement.

Sherry was handed round, and I was encouraged to take my first ever sip, like a rite of passage. It wasn't as bad as I expected, sweet and syrupy and I'd soon drained my glass, much to everyone's amusement.

My sister's new boyfriend, Eric, called round with flowers for mother, an ounce of tobacco for father and a 45 of The Shadows playing 'The Savage' for my sister.

She loved that tune. Mother played the piano in the hall and tried to pick out the melody but soon we were all singing carols.

Eric looked bemused and I'm sure he wondered what he'd walked into. He left soon after, half a schooner of sherry, two small presents he was forbidden from opening until Christmas morning, and a peck on the check from my sister better off.

After a supper of ham rolls, a boiled egg and sherry trifle we sat around the little television set they'd acquired since I'd left home.

Arthur Askey was on What's my Line and I impressed them all, even father, when I told them I'd met him backstage. Then the

Billy Cotton Band Show with my father's favourite, Eric Sykes.

The drink flowed that evening. Old differences were put aside. Even my mother took a couple of glasses of sherry.

Father broke out a whisky he'd been saving, I coughed and spluttered it over the hearth rug and everyone laughed. He got me a bottle of beer instead and we all supped in contented silence.

Father poured himself another glass of whisky, mother passed him the soda syphon and I tipped the rest of the beer into my glass.

The fire crackled and a little smoke blew back into the room. We could have sat there all night.

The cooking of the Christmas dinner had been organised with military precision. The veg was prepped, the turkey trussed up and ready to go in at 7 o'clock in the morning.

The table was set for breakfast with the lacy tablecloth we kept for special meals. There was orange juice in the refrigerator ready to accompany the eggs and bacon and beer cooling in the back yard for later.

I picked up the newspaper to see what was on the television on Christmas day. Deloris didn't take a paper. Occasionally one of her guests left one around but I'd been too busy to bother reading beyond the headlines.

Besides, I was 17, why would news from Cuba or the building of a wall in Berlin bother me?

A small article on page 5 drew my attention. I read it three times before I lowered the newspaper. I raised it again to hide my tears as my blood ran cold.

The story was about the struggles of the family of Frank Cappello who had been 'savagely bludgeoned to death in cold blood' 3 years before, while trying to save a lady from an attack on her own doorstep by the fascist Warren Bently.

'Cowardly' Warren had fled the scene and was picked up by the police while having dinner with his family the following day.

Warren, the report went on to say, 'had been executed at the gallows in Pentonville Prison in mid-December, still protesting his innocence.'

Ray Canham

The Seaside

1998

The office smelled of damp and sweat. It was really little more than an old store cupboard at the end of a corridor that led to a fire escape. The only window was high up and yellow with nicotine and dust.

Inspector Roger Mayback had been assigned to the office to review cold cases. It was, he knew, a sop, a way to ease him into retirement after arthritis meant active service was no longer an option.

A year of rifling through musty old case files in exchange for a full pension didn't fill him with delight, but after a while he found that he enjoyed picking apart evidence and statements from years ago, each one a study in the language and procedure of its time.

One case held a fascination for him, three seemingly random murders and a missing person case that might have been related. Investigations at the time concentrated on the usual suspects, locals with previous form and strangers who could have been in the area at the time.

The press had dubbed them the Seaside Murders, but only two were found at the seaside, the third in Wolverhampton and there was only the flimsiest reason to connect them; the method used by the killer.

'Look, I found this last night...' Inspector Mayback said, holding out an old photo to Chief Inspector Bagley, nominally his boss, although after years of service together the lines had become blurred.

'Yeah, not bad I suppose, I'd give her one,' he said, making to give the picture back.

'That's my mother boss. I found the picture last night going through some of her stuff.'

'Ah, sorry, still, nice looking lady your old mum.'

'Thank you, I think. Anyway, take another look, at the background.'

'Where's this then?'

'Somewhere on the East coast, Scarborough, Yarmouth maybe, around 1950 ish, that's a pier in the background and mum and dad always went to the East coast. Look at the poster on the billboard.'

The Chief Inspector put on a pair of reading glasses and peered at the picture.

'Hmmm,' he said, turning the picture over.

'It says Clacton-on-Sea, 1954 on the back. Bloody hell Rog, call yourself a detective?' He smiled at the reddening inspector as he handed the photo back.

'Just checking you're still worthy of being in charge boss. I've spent the morning checking. There are still a few gaps, and I need to cross reference some missing person reports but I think it adds up.'

***

Two weeks later the two men met in the same dingy room. One wall was now covered with photos and sticky notes. A few playbills and photos of old posters were tacked to a felt covered notice board.

'So, tell me all...' The Chief Inspector sat on the only chair in the room and smiled at Roger.

'It was the picture of my mother that gave me the clue. At the time the investigations concentrated on locals and the usual types, lorry drivers, travelling salesmen, bus drivers, even the bloody circus, but nothing quite added up.

'Eventually they were treated as isolated incidents and the conclusion was that they weren't linked.'

'And now your mum knows different?'

'And now, my mum's photo gave me

another avenue that they overlooked at the time. Actors, comedians, singers, dancers, anyone who travelled the country, especially the seaside towns.'

'Wolverhampton's a bit far from the sea Rog, even I know that, and I failed bloody geography.'

Roger sprung up from the desk where he'd been leaning.

'Exactly, so it's no end-of-the-pier specialty act, it's a name, or a crooner who does the working men's clubs, someone who travels. I thought maybe a jobbing musician, every show band needs a replacement trumpet player or drummer now and then, a session player who does the job then buggers off.'

'But?'

'But nothing I tried would quite fit, until I went through the names on the bill at Clacton.'

The Chief Inspector picked up an enlarged copy of the photo.

'If its Arthur bloody Askey we'll have a riot on our hands with the blue rinse nostalgia brigade, cheeky chappie indeed.'

'That was Max Miller.'

'Says Arthur Askey on the poster.'

'Max Miller was the Cheeky Chappie. Arthur Askey was "Big Hearted Arthur," and anyway it's not him, he was filming at

Pinewood when the second one was committed.'

'Bloody hell Rog, you actually checked up on Arthur Askey?'

'Had to eliminate him, worked down the bill, only one name could have fitted. Then I tried missing persons in the areas where they were playing and guess what?'

'Well super detective Roger Mayback, I'm going to guess by your smug demeanour and bubbling enthusiasm that you've made a match?'

'I have. I can place this chappie,' he said, pointing to a name on the bill, 'at or near the site of the murders and at least five missing persons, six or seven depending on how wide we cast the net from where he was playing... and before you ask, yes, even Wolverhampton, The Grand, 8th March 1952 as it happens.

'He stayed for three nights at the Palace Guest House, long gone of course.'

'Motive?'

'They wanted to build a block of flats there.'

'Motive for the murders, not Wolverhampton bloody council's town planning department Rog.'

'Nothing obvious yet. But the three murdered men we can link all had their throats cut...' the Chief Inspector cut him off by waving the enlarged photo.

'As I recall, they didn't just have their throats cut, they were slashed and torn and the coroner concluded that the assailant used a very small knife, a pen knife or vegetable knife maybe. Something that is easy to conceal until the right moment.'

'That's what the original team thought. The victims were probably drugged though, a mild tranquilliser readily available and most likely administered in a drink.'

'Okay, so this chappie can be placed at or near the scenes, was in the vicinity of some mis-pers, but has he any form, anything to suggest it's not just coincidence?'

'No, nothing we can find, a pretty blameless if somewhat nomadic life.'

'Any relatives to chase up?'

'None we can trace.'

Then I doubt we've got enough to get it signed off Rog. Great work and all that but without some sort of proof it'll just be suspicion and noted on the files as such. Sorry mate, I think it's a dead end.'

'Unless...' said Roger, opening a slim manilla folder, 'We ask him.'

'He can't still be alive?'

'94, apparently still breathing and not doo-lally, although the bloke in charge of the home where he lives would rather we didn't use that term. He was quite emphatic as it happens.

'Our man is currently residing in Eastbourne, some place for retired theatrical types.'

***

The following morning was overcast, dark clouds hung over the sea and the roads were still slick from the overnight rain.

Detective Mayback and Chief Inspector Bagley presented themselves to the receptionist, who caught the attention of a passing nursing assistant.

'Oh, Sharon, would you be a love and show these gentlemen to room 12 please.'

Sharon led them upstairs and along a corridor lined with neatly framed old playbills and film posters. The Chief Inspector silently pointed out an old poster to his colleague.

For one night only!
****

The Empire Ballroom,
Morcombe-on-Sea presents:
The man with the biggest heart in showbusiness

Mr Arthur Askey
Stars of Stage & Screen
Dorren and Alan Cartwright
Performing songs from 'The Last Train' and many other smash hits
****

Mr Peter Fraser & the cheeky Bobby Baxter
Burton 'The Chipper Chappie' Coggles
Vince the Magnificent with the belle of the Orient Suzie Wong
Your compere – the dapper
Mr Kirk Smeaton!
****

Introducing Mr Desmond O'Connor
Featuring The Sally Preston Dancers
The Fabulous Mills Brothers
And Sammy the Witch Doctor

When she reached the door Sharon turned to the two detectives.

'Here we are gents, room 12. He'll be up and about by now; do you want me to introduce you?'

'We'll be fine love, thank you,' the Chief Inspector said. They waited for her to leave them alone.

'Do the honours please Roger, this is your case,' he said, stepping aside for the inspector to knock on the door.

When the formalities were over Roger sat on the only other chair while the Chief Inspector perched awkwardly on the side of the bed. The man opposite him was gaunt but neatly dressed in a linen suit with a loose cravat at his neck. He appeared quite sprightly and on the ball. Roger would have put him at a fit 75 – 80 rather than his 90 plus years.

'We'd like to ask you a few questions about some old cases we've been working on.'

'Certainly Inspector.'

'You may recall the seaside murders from the papers some time ago? Three young men, all murdered in a similar fashion. There are also a few missing persons who might be linked.'

The man looked up with milky white eyes. Gripping the arms of his chair he leaned forward for a moment then let himself slump back and seemed to shrink into his chair.

He stared out of the window for a moment then turned back to the Inspector.

'Ah, yes indeed. I think it's about time it all came out. I couldn't betray him you know.'

The two detectives briefly made eye contact. Roger very slowly and deliberately asked.

'Betray whom Mr Fraser?'

'The person you want is there, in that suitcase. He didn't approve of my, er, dalliances. Going behind Cindy's back. Affairs I suppose you'd call them.

'With men too, he really didn't understand, poor thing and he can become quite spiteful. Can't say I blame him really.

'Bobby, I think it's finally time you came out to face the music dear chap,' he said, slowly removing the puppet from its suitcase.

The Weight of Sin

Ray Canham

The Palace Ballroom, Skegness

'Ladies and gentlemen, fresh from a sell-out season in Scarborough, we are proud to present the Chipper Chappie himself, please give a big welcome to Mr Burton Coggles!'

'Thank you, Kirk.

'Good evening ladies and gentlemen.

'Come on, I know you're out there, I can hear you breathing.

'Testing 1,2, 4...testing 1,2, 4...hey is this microphone leaking, where's the 3 gone?

'Talking of number 3, I learnt an interesting fact today, did you know ladies and gents, did you know that there are only three types of people in the world? ...those who can count and those who can't...

'Now, you can see me, but I can't see you. Can we have the house lights up Reg? That's Reg on lights ladies and gents...

'Lovely chap is our Reg. He used to be in the army, trained as a karate expert, he had to leave the service though, he used to knock himself out every time he saluted.

'That's better, thank you Reg now I can see you all. Let me have a look down here in the front row...

'Good evening, sir, that's a fine hat you've got there balanced on your leg. Is it a knee-cap?

'What's your name sir? Lance. That's not a common name these days. Of course, in medieval times people were named Lance a lot.

'What is it you do Lance?

'A book dealer. Wow. What sort of books do you deal in Lance?

'Old ones. That helps.

'I've quite a library at home you might be surprised to learn that, Lance. Yes indeed, I'll tell you what Lance, I've nearly finished colouring in another one.

'I say Lance, do you have any Kipling?

'You do? That's grand that is. This fellow the other day asked me if I liked Kipling? I said how do I know? - I've never kippled.

'Is this your wife Lance?

'No? Goodness, maybe I should move on... Oh it's your daughter, well that's a relief.

'My optician had a daughter who looked a bit like you love, mind you, she did make a spectacle of herself.

'Is he a good father?

'He is, that's splendid. Well done Lance.

'My dad was a good un. He used to tell me to go to bed because the cows were sleeping in the field. He'd say, "It's pasture bedtime Burton!"

'Moving along, oh, hello Madam, I see you've decided to join us, have a seat. What kept you?

'The queue to powder your nose? Really? You shouldn't get them to queue up to powder your nose for you dear.

'Talking of queues, this chap went to the front of the queue at the butchers. Straight to the front. I said to him, hey mister, go to the back of the queue. Do you know what he said?

'He said "I went to the back but there was already somebody there!"

'Cheeky so and so.

'When I got to the front I asked the butcher for a large sausage, he said, "certainly Burton it won't be long," I said, "well it had better be wide then!"

'I asked him if he could show me how to make a sausage roll, he said, "Of course I can Burton, just push it down a hill."

'I bet him he couldn't reach the meat on the top shelf. He said he wasn't going to bet with me, told me the steaks were too high.

'Now, where was I?

'I bought some bees from the market. Thought I'd start a little hive, so I paid for a dozen. The bloke gave me thirteen, said the extra was a free bee.

'My Maud, she doesn't like insects.

Hates them she does. She found a spider in the bedroom, Ug! It had ten eyes...Ten! Do you know what you call a spider with 10 eyes madam?

'A Sp-i-i-i-i-i-i-i-i-i-der.

'Won't find any creepy crawlies in this place, will you? It is posh here, isn't it? Look at that great big chandelier, that's a high-light!

'I don't know about you, but I feel a bit out of place in this sort of gaff. Lance looks at home down the front don't you Lance? Nice whistle and flute, bet that didn't come from the Red Cross did it eh? What's that little badge on your lapel?

'Arsenal Football Club! Arsenal, cor blimey, you're a long way from home Lance.

'I had two Arsenal tickets on my mantlepiece back at home. Some beggar broke in and do you know what he did Lance? He left another two with them!

'Their manager Tom Whittaker he's a tough nut. He caught two fans climbing over the wall, gave em' a right telling off and told them to get back in and watch the rest of the game.

'Where were we? Oh' yes, it is a lot posher in here than my digs.

'I knocked on the door and this lady stuck her head out of the window and said,

"What do you want?"

'I said, "I'd like to stay here please misses."

'She said, "Well, stay there then," and closed the window!

'Then she told me I had to make my own bed - and gave me a bundle of wood and a box of nails.

'She said did I want a room with a bath or a shower? I said what's the difference. She said you stand up in the shower...Well, honestly...

'Oh, before I go, I almost forgot...There's these two fish in a tank, one turns to the other and says, "Hey, how do you drive this thing?"

"Burton...Burton...Time to wake up love, time for your pills...Burton...Burton!

'That's all from me you've been a super audience, thank you and goodnight.'

A Personal Reflection.

As I said in the introduction, I warm towards the loners and 'little people'. The ones who keep the world ticking over while others take the glory. I suppose that's how I see civil servants, neat people in sensible footwear beavering away at all hours because they have no life outside of work. I'm sure that in reality many are sexy beasts overflowing with charisma and erotic allure. Probably.

Reflecting on characters like Len, or the father in The Savage, even Mr Jones, I see quite a bit of my father in them. He was born to accountancy like a fish is born to swim. Intelligent, wry and sprightly but very much a behind the scenes person. Of course he wasn't, as far as I'm aware, a hangman or time travelling assassin. He certainly didn't enjoy punk like Len grew to, although I do recall he was impressed by the drummer of Stiff Little Fingers on their version of Bob Marleys Johnny Was, right before asking me, for the umpteenth time, to turn it down.

As a child I really wanted him to be a hero. To have some secret life tucked away in his briefcase as he left for work at 7.25am prompt. I wished the Reliant Owners Club (yes, we really did have a 3-wheeled fibreglass deathtrap), was a ruse and actually he was a spy or international jewel thief.

Which, with hindsight, was terribly unfair. He'd seen active service in the navy, was an accomplished musician and drum and bugle tutor with the Boys Brigade, had been a champion gymnast and brought up my sister after his first wife died following childbirth. He also had a sense of fun as a fan of The Goons and, of course, old music hall variety acts. He'd have loved Burton Goggles.

The Savage is set around 1958. Burtons story started at around the same time, although his story spans several generations, I started it from the middle and filled in his story from that point. This is an era I've researched a lot about thanks to my mother's diary's, which is explained in detail in my book The Mitchley Waltz.

The late 50's was a time of change and The Savage exemplifies the tensions and contradictions of the time. The rise of fascism, racial tensions that would spill over into the Notting Hill Riots, the beginning of the end of the Death Penalty, traditional structures being challenged by the rise of the teenager, with disposable income and free time, and homosexuality still a crime.

Burtons world would have been in decline, cinema and increasingly television was keeping his audiences away, and dancing was taking off with the 45rpm record on the market being sold to teenagers in ever increasing numbers. They wanted their own world of up-tempo music, skiffle, rock and roll, and out from that scene in the early 60s beat combos like The Beatles would emerge to change the world. As did the Shadows of course, backing Cliff Richard but also producing their own hits like The Savage to a familiar formula. All the time Burtons style of variety show was being squeezed out to the provinces and seaside shows where nostalgia ruled and anything was better than a windy afternoon on Morcombe beach waiting for the boarding house landlady to let you back in.

Of the other stories, The Wilderness expresses the mundane, albeit with a twist. It came about after I overheard conversation that spiralled in my head into a tale of two rather ordinary people settled comfortably into a groove that hasn't changed for years. Quite what Lucy, and her brother many years earlier, do that tips the balance is anyone's guess, although money issues would appear to be at the root of their displeasure.

The Coffee Hut is another example of an observation that takes root and becomes a story. It's a bit of an oddity, I hadn't expected to incorporate anything supernatural but something about the lady I'd seen at the coffeeshop in Waterloo station seemed otherworldly. I'm not sure quite who the lady in my story is, an angel maybe, some harvester of souls perhaps, death his, or rather her, self? Or perhaps she is just a little old lady who goes to meet a group of children. Who knows?

I never feel the need to complete the picture for the reader. Whoever she is, and what her motivation is for saving Simon might be, that's up to you, the reader. The same goes for The Stirk, who knows what becomes of the protagonist? Did he find the Stirk and if so, how will he get off? Over to you...

The Weight of Sin is a story that examines many of my fears. I have recurring dreams about being executed. The biggest concern upon waking is the calm detachment of everyone around me in the dream. This awful, ritualised death awaits and people are planning holidays, watering the plants, ordering pizza or discussing the weather. The method of execution used in The Weight of Sin is from a nightmare I've had a few times, its percolated in my head and finally found an outlet.

My other nightmare, but this time one I have when I'm awake, is a totalitarian government. In this scenario its ultra-right wing, but it could equally be the wests equivalent of Mao, Stalin, or Pol Pot. The idea that power can rest unopposed and impose their moral code upon everyone must be resisted. It's the same argument if people invoke the Koran or The Bible, or even Marx. Take from them by all means, live your life according to the moral code you believe in but leave it to individuals to make their own choice. To wield power based on theocracy is, I think, abhorrent.

I'm sure a psychologist would have a field day with The Weight of Sin and my explanation thereof. Poor Michael would have been better off studying my dreams than getting involved with the Whitehall mob. The first draft of this was Michael's story, but I felt it lacked a satisfactory ending. I knew that the deal would be the lynchpin of the narrative, but it wasn't until I introduced another perspective, that of the criminal, that the tale started to coalesce. Having Mr Jones pop up was an indulgence on my part. I rather like him and thought he'd enjoy being involved.

Cheese and Pickle Sandwiches is another that started life in parts. Three linked but separate stories came together over a period of around a year, and here I must pay tribute to Alison for tireless editing and advice to help me meld it into one continuous story. What you have read is my responsibility so any continuity errors or dubious plot devices are entirely mine. There are sly references to the Book of Revelations (the four horsemen, the white (pale) horse ridden by Death, the 7 portals which could be likened to the 7 seals, for example) that suggest it might be a biblical apocalypse, but then again...

The Man Who Spoke to No One is an indulgence. It is a whimsical observation shoehorned into the book for want of anywhere else to go. It is though, a serious subject and the digital age is excluding more and more people while supposedly making life easier. Loneliness kills, especially older people. Health risks are many and varied, including those associated with inactivity like high blood pressure, obesity and lower immune function, and psychological effects include low self-esteem and poor coping mechanisms like smoking and poor diet. Studies have shown links to Alzheimer's and lower life expectancy.

So, if you take nothing else away from this book, please say hello to that older relative you keep meaning to call but never seem to quite get around to it.

The Seaside rounds off the main body of stories. I rather like the detectives, even though two wisecracking policemen is a cliché I hope you'll forgive me using them as a tool to expose Peter, or Bobbies, exploits. Of course I wanted you to think it was Burton all along, but I couldn't do that to him.

It would be like writing a sex scene for Mr Jones, some things you just don't do.

Burtons finale rounds off the book and I think it's appropriate he bookends proceedings. I had his act worked out but the inclusion of the nurse trying to rouse him was a very late addition. I knew something was needed. If in doubt, add pathos.

Ideas come before accuracy in my early drafts, so I find writing increasingly frustrating as rewrites, edits and other necessary evils drag on. Every time I finally get to start the publishing process, I swear it'll be the last time. I spoke those very words recently and promised myself this would be my last book.

Then I found an article about an old ferry plying between the Hebridean Islands that was built and equipped to be hastily commandeered to serve as an emergency headquarters for essential personnel in the event of nuclear war. This was a gift to a writer who lived through the cold war, when every household was issued with Protect and Survive, a government instruction manual on how to keep safe in the event of a nuclear strike.

There is a story in there, maybe a whole book, who knows...

Ray Canham

May 2024

Acknowledgments.

First and foremost, with every book I write I am increasingly in debt to Alison for her encouragement, editing and general superness.

Thanks to Andy, Tracey, Louise, Mel, Pauline and Karen for reading early drafts of some of these stories and giving feedback. Also, a special mention for Barry, the inspiration for Barry 'Baz' Butler.

Most of these stories have a genesis somewhere in the real world. What happens between inspiration and the finished story is an enormous leap of imagination, which is my way of saying that, to the best of my knowledge, none of the people who inspired these stories is a killer or in any way associated with nefarious activities, 'dad jokes', the reaping of souls or setting off the apocalypse.

About the author.

Born in London and raised in Hertfordshire and Suffolk, Ray was drifting through high school until he discovered punk rock. From then on, he spent his time nurturing his lack of musical ability, until realising too late that exam success might have been a better option. Despite his abysmal school exam results, he went on to forge a career as a nurse, such was the desperation of the NHS in the early 80s.

After a second career in Social Housing and Community Development he and Alison left the rat race, swapped their house for a motorhome and took to the open road.

Life on the road re-ignited a desire to write, which despite the best efforts of his teachers had never been extinguished. His previous writing experience includes company annual reports, a punk rock fanzine and forging notes from his mother to excuse him from PE.

In 2018 he published his first book,

Downwardly Mobile, documenting his and Alison's escape from the rat race and spending the best part of 2016 on the road, working at festivals and discovering the UK from the vantage point of a Motorhome called Mavis.

'You could imagine yourself looking out of the window and seeing it with your own eyes, such was the way it was described. Be prepared to laugh out loud, I got some funny looks when reading this on the bus when I would chuckle and then cry in equal measure. Be sure to read this book.'

After moving to the Isle of Mull and living in their motorhome, Ray published the next instalment of his and Alison's adventures in Still Following Rainbows.

It documents the highs and lows of adjusting to life and work on Mull. With snippets of history and vivid descriptions of the landscape you'll feel like you're along for the ride, and with Ray's insightful observations of people, places and situations this book will produce tears and explosions of laughter in equal measure.

"I cannot recommend this book highly enough. Ray is a gifted storyteller, and his words have the power to draw out a whole range of emotions as we journey with himself, Alison, and Mavis to a new life on a Scottish island. It's real, it's raw and it will make you want to visit Mull!"

At the beginning of the lockdown in 2020 Ray decided to do his bit for the Covid-19 lockdown and raid his scrap book for unpublished articles, short stories and pieces cut from his other books as an economy-priced diversion for everyone stuck at home. So, he published Even Unicorns Die - a collection of short stories, articles and assorted nonsense.

"Wow! This is very different from Ray's autobiographical writing: be warned! It's a delight to read - but don't let that fool you into expectations of a collection of lightweight, heart-warming, feel-good fuzz. This writing has depth and darkness. There are political observations, stories with unexpected stings, thought-provoking reflections, hellish humour, and an alphabet rhyme which you wouldn't want anywhere near your children! It's good. Very good! Order a copy at once!"

Rays writing in 2020 went from the ridiculous to the sublime with the publication of The Mitchley Waltz.

As the country was finally recovering from war, Rays mother was a young woman living in North London. The family were just recovering from her parents' divorce when she received a grim diagnosis. She recorded the events that changed her life in her diaries as she was prescribed bed rest, confined to hospital and then a long convalescence.

Trying to make the best of her confinement Iris she had to face the fear that her blossoming career as a ballroom dancing instructor may now be over, along with any possibility of finding love with any of her potential suitors.

As the years passed, the diaries recorded her personal traumas and anxieties, her dreams and ambitions and they revealed a survivor who faced her worries with a steely determination and fought to overcome the legacy of permanent frailty.

Ignoring medical advice and returning to the dancefloor, could she ever make her dreams a reality, and could she risk opening her heart to the shy widower who had started attending her classes?

After her death in 2018, Ray found her diaries among her possessions and set about transcribing them. Along with additional research and commentary he has brought the London that Iris knew in the 1950s back to life in vivid Technicolour.

"It's an excellent time capsule of life around that time, made all the more poignant by the true story of one woman's trials and brought to life with the author's scene setting and accompanying footnotes."

In 2023 Ray had two books published that couldn't have been more diverse. First to hit the shelves, or rather shelf, as its exclusive to Duart Castle on the Isle of Mull, was A Short History of the Life of Sir Fitzroy Maclean.

Ray was given exclusive access to the castle records and Sir Fitzroy's personal papers to edit his journals. They tell the fascinating story of a gentleman and solider very much of his time, who was born during the reign of King William IV in 1835 and saw action during the Crimea War, where he had first hand experience of The Charge of the Light Brigade and retired at 75 years old to restore the ancient seat of the Clan Maclean, Duart Castle on the Isle of Mull, living their until his death in 1936 at the age of 101.

Using a pseudonym that would fool no one, he also published The Revolution Will be Televised, a passionate and humorous look at modern society from a left-field anarchist perspective.

"Smart, funny and easily digestible, The Revolution Will Be Televised *is a voice of reason in an age of unreason...The author clearly understands that change...however narrow, is imperative, that righteous rallying cries of protest and anger will only carry us so far. Empathy is a fast-disappearing trait but it's here in spades, the decks cleared to offer something a little more realistic. That it is done with alacrity, warmth, and a cheeky sense of humour transforms what could have been a despairing rant into a revitalising pep-talk."*

RAY STUART

Ray wrote 'The Revolution Will Be Televised' because he finally realised that if our present government wasn't going to trigger open rebellion, then nothing would.

Instead, he has embraced his middle-class roots; where he used to be full of passion and rage, he is now full of artisan bread and locally sourced cheese. Meat may be murder but so are his knees. He's leaving the street fighting and statue tipping to the young. Instead 'The Revolution Will Be Televised' is an appeal to people from all backgrounds, to imagine and work for a better, fairer society without the reliance on the straightjackets of traditional left-right politics or inherited privilege.

An important book in changing times, available now, direct from Earth Island Books, or any good book or record shop, or online retailer.

Remember, in this age of media, 'The Revolution Will Be Televised'.

A HARDCORE HEAR

Adventures in a D.I.Y. sce

David is a 'lifer' - he's been around the block and earnt his stripes – and
Hardcore Heart' is not only a fascinating insight into the reality of tourir
with an underground hardcore band, but an invigorating time capsule of
punk scene before Instagram, Facebook and MySpace, even before mobi
phones, sat navs and Google Maps. It's a veritable ode to being in the wror
place at the wrong time, an underdog story with (spoiler alert!) no happ
ending, yet that won't stop its bittersweet narrative from putting a wry smi
on your face.
Ian Glasper- Down For Life (and author of 'The Scene That Would Not Die'

Want to know what it was really like to submerge yourself in the nineties Har
core scene? To live, eat, breathe, and be consumed by punk rock? Or what th
reality of being in a touring band that lived hand to mouth and played mo
shows than the author cares to, or probably can remember, for the sheer jo
of playing and not a whole lot else? Then you need to read 'A Hardcore Hear
a book that's a love letter to the intoxicating joy of music, the enduring pow
of friendship, loyalty, and the overwhelming desire to create something fro
nothing and forge a better tomorrow. Thoroughly recommended.
Tim Cundle – Mass Movement (and author of 'What Would Gary Gygax Do

AN ARCHIST ATHEIST PUNK ROCK TEACHER

(A Memoir of Struggle, Grief, Philosophy and Hope)
By DaN McKee

Exploring the various ways in which anarchist philosophy, atheism, and a background in DIY punk rock influenced one conflicted teacher's approach to the classroom over twelve turbulent and thought-provoking years, 'Anarchist Atheist Punk Rock Teacher' is more than just a memoir of some teacher you've never met. It is philosophy of education, of anarchism, of authenticity, and of life. Throw in some personal history, the deaths of both of his parents to deal with on top of juggling all the professional absurdities that come with the job (not to mention having to teach through a global pandemic), and you have all the earmarks of a biographical classic.

A COUNTRY FIT FOR HEROES
DIY PUNK IN EIGHTIES BRITAIN BY IAN GLASP[ER]

Primarily collecting the stories of over 140 UK punk bands from the eighties who on[ly]
released EPs and demos, or only appeared on compilation LPs, 'A Country Fit for Hero[es]
DIY punk in eighties Britain' is a celebration of the obscure, a love letter to the UK
punk underground.

'A Country Fit For Heroes' plugs the gaps in Ian Glasper's first three books on UK p[unk]
in the eighties, performing a truly deep dive into that volatile subculture to create [a]
more complete historical document of a most turbulent time.

With a foreword by Chris Berry, co-founder of No Future Records, this is an essential [read]
for anyone with more than a passing interest in the UK's grass roots punk scene.

AVAILABLE NOW AT: WWW.EARTHISLANDBOOKS.COM

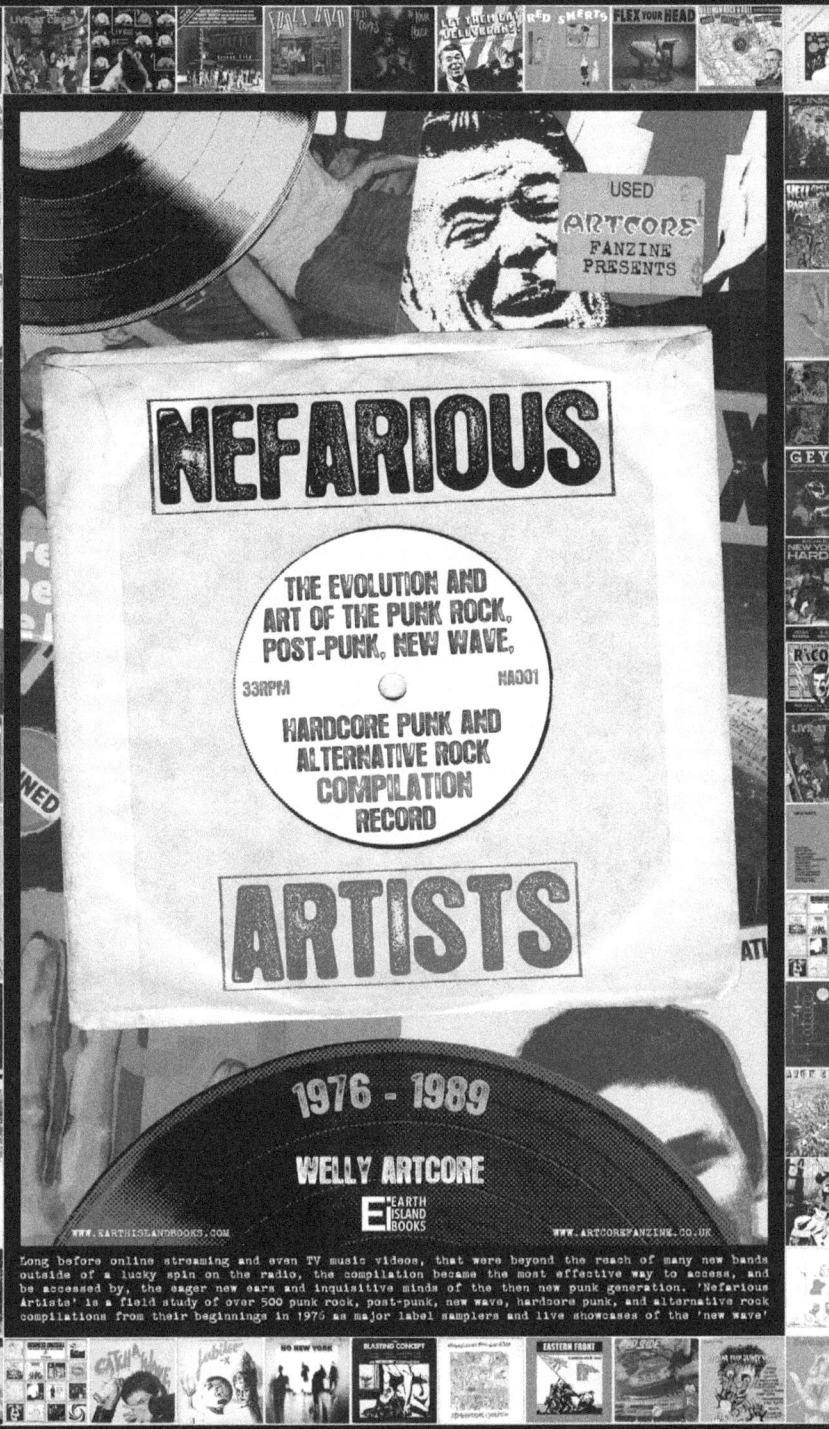

ARTCORE
FANZINE
PRESENTS

NEFARIOUS

THE EVOLUTION AND ART OF THE PUNK ROCK, POST-PUNK, NEW WAVE,

33RPM   NA001

HARDCORE PUNK AND ALTERNATIVE ROCK COMPILATION RECORD

ARTISTS

1976 - 1989

WELLY ARTCORE

E EARTH ISLAND BOOKS

WWW.EARTHISLANDBOOKS.COM   WWW.ARTCOREFANZINE.CO.UK

Long before online streaming and even TV music videos, that were beyond the reach of many new bands outside of a lucky spin on the radio, the compilation became the most effective way to access, and be accessed by, the eager new ears and inquisitive minds of the then new punk generation. 'Nefarious Artists' is a field study of over 500 punk rock, post-punk, new wave, hardcore punk, and alternative rock compilations from their beginnings in 1976 as major label samplers and live showcases of the 'new wave'

Milton Keynes UK
Ingram Content Group UK Ltd.
UKHW050203091124
450928UK00019B/220

9 781916 864320